Roger Longrigg was a British au
wrote both novels and non-fiction, a
for television, under both his own na   ... . pseudonyms,
including *Laura Black, Ivor Drummond, Domini Taylor,* and *Frank
Parish.*

Born in Edinburgh into a military family, he was at first schooled in
the Middle East, but returned to England as a youth and later read
history at Magdalen College, Oxford. His early career took him into
advertising, but after the publication of two comic novels he took up
writing full time in 1959.

He completed fifty five books, many under his own name, but also
Scottish historical fiction as *Laura Black*; thrillers as *Ivor Drummond*;
black comedies as *Domini Taylor*; and famously *Rosalind Erskine* – a
name with which he hoaxed all for several years – who appeared to
write a disguised biography of what life was like in a girls boarding
school where, with classmates, she ran a brothel for boys from a
nearby school. 'The Passion Flower Hotel' became a bestseller and
was later filmed.

Roger Longrigg's work in television included '*Mother Love*', a BBC
mini-series starring Diana Rigg and David McCallum, and episodes
of '*Crown Court*' and '*Dial M for Murder*'. He died in 2000, aged
70, and was survived by his wife, the novelist Jane Chichester, and
three daughters.

Works by Roger Longrigg
Published by House of Stratus

BABE IN THE WOOD
BAD BET
DAUGHTERS OF MULBERRY
THE DESPERATE CRIMINALS
A HIGH PITCHED BUZZ
THE JEVINGTON SYSTEM
LOVE AMONG THE BOTTLES
THE PAPER BOATS
THE SUN ON THE WATER
SWITCHBOARD
THEIR PLEASING SPORT
WRONG NUMBER

AS LAURA BLACK:
ALBANY
CASTLE RAVEN
FALLS OF GARD
GLENDRACO
STRATHGALLANT

AS IVOR DRUMMOND:
THE DIAMONDS OF LORETA
THE FROG IN THE MOONFLOWER
THE JAWS OF THE WATCHDOG
THE MAN WITH THE TINY HEAD
THE NECKLACE OF SKULLS
THE POWER OF THE BUG
THE PRIESTS OF THE ABOMINATION
THE STENCH OF POPPIES
THE TANK OF SACRED EELS

AS FRANK PARISH:
BAIT ON THE HOOK
CAUGHT IN THE BIRDLIME
FACE AT THE WINDOW
FIRE IN THE BARLEY
FLY IN THE COBWEB
SNARE IN THE DARK
STING OF THE HONEYBEE

AS DOMINI TAYLOR:
THE EYE BEHIND THE CURTAIN
GEMINI
MOTHER LOVE
NOT FAIR
PRAYING MANTIS
SIEGE
SUFFER LITTLE CHILDREN
THE TIFFANY LAMP

AS ROSALIND ERSKINE
THE PASSION FLOWER HOTEL

The Passion
Flower Hotel

Roger Longrigg
(Writing as Rosalind Erskine)

HOUSE OF
STRATUS

This edition published in 2014 by House of Stratus, an imprint of Stratus Books Ltd., Lisandra House, Fore Street, Looe, Cornwall, PL13 1AD, UK.

www.houseofstratus.com

Typeset by House of Stratus.

A catalogue record for this book is available from the British Library and the Library of Congress.

ISBN 07551-0503-6
EAN 978-07551-0503-8

Chapter One

I was very nearly fifteen when I read Virginia's book about prostitution. So I was quite old enough not to be influenced by it. In any case, we all discussed it a good deal (at night, of course, but also on walks, and drinking packaged soup we made, and during rehearsals for the Play), and I find that discussing things makes them lose their influence. I find the same with Shelley and Dylan Thomas and the Georgians.

> *Taken by light in her arms at long and dear last*
> *I may without fail*
> *Suffer the first vision that set fire to the stars.*

That seems to me enough to influence anybody. I was quite clear, after I read it a few times and learned it, that as soon as I was in love I would take him in my arms *by light*. But we discussed it (Mary-Rose and Melissa and Janet and Virginia and I) and I saw that, of course, the whole thing might turn out to be different. For all sorts of reasons: it would be night, probably, and if *he* said 'Shall I put the light out?' what would he think if I said 'No?' Virginia pointed this out; and then Melissa and Mary-Rose had an argument about whether men liked girls they thought were tarty, regardless of whether the girls actually were tarty or not. Melissa said they liked girls that *were* actually tarty, but the men didn't realise it.

'Not in my experience,' said Mary-Rose.

'Ha ha, *your* experience.'

'At a party last holidays.'

'Well, tell us.'

1

'I'm not certain I want to.'

'*Sacred*, Mary-Rose?'

'Important to me.'

'Of course, we wouldn't,' said Janet expectantly, 'want to intrude on anything you hold precious.'

'Oh, all right,' said Mary-Rose. 'Well, I was wearing my blue with those thin straps. We did one of those reels, and I was dancing with this *much* older boy—'

'How much older?'

'Sixteen and a half at least. Or *more.*'

'Voice?'

'Bass.'

'Shave?'

'Every other day at least.'

'Spots?'

'A few, but only on the back of his neck.'

'All right, you were dancing this reel. *And then?*'

'One of the straps kept slipping down over my shoulder.'

'Just by itself?'

'The thing is, if I lean forward when the straps are *up*, it's all right. But if one of them's down, I think you can see my bosom.'

'Tour *bosom,* Mary-Rose?'

'My left, in this case.'

'But you haven't got a bosom.'

'I most certainly have.'

'Not compared to Sarah,' said Janet.

'Leave me out of this,' I said. But it is true. I have got a bosom.

'Or even compared to me,' said Melissa.

'I most emphatically have more bosom than you,' said Mary-Rose.

'Pneumatically,' I said.

'Bet?' said Melissa.

'Sixpence.'

'Done.'

They took off their sweaters and vests (we were out on a walk, so this was a bit chilly and risky) and we measured them. Janet had a tape-measure. Janet has everything, except, *I* think, sex-appeal. Mary-Rose won: it was thirty-three to thirty-two and a half.

'I think you both have beautiful breasts,' said Virginia.

'Virginia!'

'Can't you tell the difference between politeness and lesbianism?'

'Yes, I can. What worries me is, can you?'

Presently they were dressed again and Janet said, '*So,* Mary-Rose? He saw your breast and *then* what?'

'After supper he took me outside. It was very warm and almost dark and the stars were beginning to show—'

'That's enough *Woman's Own,* thanks. What did he say in his great bass voice?'

'Nothing. He kissed me quite silently.'

'On the mouth?'

'Just beside Actually, I think he missed.'

'Open or shut?' I said.

'What do you mean, Sarah?'

'If you don't know yet,' I said, 'I wouldn't want the responsibility of telling you.'

'Go on, Mary-Rose,' said Janet. I had a feeling Janet's sex-life would always be lived vicariously.

'Well, he put his hand on my front.'

'Outside your dress?'

'First of all.'

'*So then?*'

He had wanted to kiss it, Mary-Rose claimed, but she refused to say whether she had let him or not. I personally did not believe this story, although I pretended to. But it was dreadful to think that it *might have been true.* I am far more advanced, physically and emotionally, than Mary-Rose, and nothing like that had ever happened to me. Nothing remotely like that.

Anyway, the influence of 'Taken by light in her arms' got totally eroded by all this. As always – it was exactly the same with *Lolita.* Virginia brought a copy back at the beginning of the winter term, and we all read it before we discussed it. We agreed that the situation was feasible, but it was irrelevant to our own lives. Lolita was younger (though physically precocious) and much more naive. All those sweets and comics – we got over most sweets and things like *Girl* the term before last. The real difference is being European. I personally am extremely European. Even Virginia, who is Jewish and rather cosmopolitan, is no more utterly European than I am.

(On some things I take a totally mature view. If anyone said to me: 'Do you like Jews?' I should reply: 'Do you like people with red hair?' This is, I think, mature. But no one has ever asked me this question, or any of the others I have got good answers ready for.)

One *Lolita* discussion we had was in a yellowish place called the History Library. We belonged to Form 5B, to which I personally felt no sense of loyalty. Form 5B was allowed in the History Library. It had books and a table, and quite comfortable chairs, and half a huge window. (The other half lit the Senior Day-Room; the two rooms had been one when the house was a house, and painted in pretty colours, and there were flowers in the rooms and no notice-boards, or fear, or lavatories with incomplete doors like loose-boxes.) The best thing in the History Library was an electric fire which you could turn on its back. On this we made soup from packets. Many of my best remarks were first uttered there. Other members of 5B sometimes tried to get into the History Library when we were talking there. We dealt with them depending. A girl called Lydia Radcliffe we beat up. Johnson-Johnson we froze. Anne-Louise Campion we shocked. Fat slob Jennifer Bostwicke we did something exceptional to, which Janet thought up. (Janet has rather a dirty mind.) They all went back to the Senior Day-Room, where they belonged. We were very unpopular and anti-social and domineering, and this got us by.

'For instance,' said Mary-Rose, drinking her Mixed Vegetable a bit greedily, 'she took utterly the whole entire initiative that first time.'

'Cheapening,' said Janet.

'One has a certain pride.'

'No man I know,' said Melissa, 'would think the same of me.'

'When you say *know*, Melissa—?'

'My measurements may be less bloated than some, but I too have shoulder-straps.'

'Why?'

'What we all need,' said Virginia, with very European tact, 'is a situation where we don't have to take the initiative, and yet—'

'And yet be certain—'

'Be certain they're thinking along the same lines—'

'There ought to be a specialised kind of Universal Aunts,' said Melissa.

'Universal Procureuses,' said Virginia. I must admit she can pronounce the French 'R' very well. I can too, as it happens, but I always feel shy about it. If I were in France, with nobody English listening, my R's would gurgle sexily, practically from my diaphragm.

'Yes,' said Mary-Rose thoughtfully, 'what one wants is to be somewhere comfortable—'

'Darkish—'

'Warmish—'

'And you both know—'

'Without having to say so—'

'Somebody should set up an organisation.'

'It would be a service.'

'I'd almost pay.'

'They'd pay, I'm sure.'

'Boys? God, yes. Any amount.'

'In advance,' I murmured.

And at that moment, I think, I had the Idea.

* * *

Five is an awkward number for a set. Melissa and Janet were each other's greatest friends, and in a funnier way so were Mary-Rose and Virginia. I was the greatest friend of each of them, *after* whichever it was, but I was definitely not, personally, any one person's greatest friend. Perhaps this is a sign of my greater maturity. Sometimes, as on Set Walks, it was a nuisance, and sad. But it had certain advantages. If Melissa, for instance, had an idea, Janet would support it automatically, but Mary-Rose would always oppose it. But if I had a plan I could nearly always, in the end, get it accepted by them all.

Not that I had a plan *yet* – not all at once in the History Library. Just the beginnings of the Idea. But I remember looking round them and thinking: what they want they shall have!

Mary-Rose wore a greenish sweater (because she had reddish hair), and she was looking at her empty soup cup, with the rather cross expression she often has – pouting, almost. Her hair is a bit dry-looking, but she is definitely sexy. Virginia was next to her, in a cashmere (at school!); she had that brooding look which I suppose is racial. She has marvellous bones and eyes and a sort of wiriness. Undoubtedly sexy. Then Janet, fussing with the saucepan. Janet is Scottish and rather freckly. She has wonderful legs, and takes a lot of trouble, but I think she would be a special taste. With Janet it would be like rape *every time.* Perhaps this would be attractive to a certain type of man. And Melissa – Melissa would be a case of *nostalgie de la boue.* She is dark, and her hair is greasy-looking even if she shampoos twice a week. Also she can't seem to keep her finger-nails quite clean, which is why she is dying to be old enough to varnish. Eager. Very sexy.

'Oh God,' said Melissa, 'it's raining again.'

'No hockey, thank God.'

'Bloody Set Walk.'

'Blossom will wear her plastic hood,' said Virginia.

'Out of it will poke her little grey sausage curls.'

'Bedewed with bloody rai-hai-hain,' sang Melissa. 'I shall run away and work in a strip-club.'

'What as?' said Mary-Rose.

'You'd do better,' I said quietly, 'in a strip-cartoon.'

"Which one, funny-pants?'

'*Peanuts.*'

Melissa threw a book at me but I ducked sinuously and it crashed against the wall. The pages came out of the binding all in a block. The binding, on its own, looked useful for something – I wasn't sure what. Janet put it together again and started reading it. Melissa walked up and down, practising walks. When she wiggled her behind she couldn't stick her chest out, and when she stuck her chest out, her behind got all clenched and stiff. Mary-Rose and Virginia sang 'John Henry'. I thought about us all and marked us out of ten for sex-appeal:

Me: 10 out of 10
Virginia: 8
Melissa: 7
Mary-Rose: 7
Janet: 4

With a *black* man it would probably be different. Janet would be 6 or even 9.

Presently the bell went for the end of Break and we went to a room called 'Thackeray' for English.

I am by far the best at English, not just of our set but in the whole form (This is not vanity, but realistic) Also I have large dark-blue eyes and an excellent figure My name is Sarah Callender. My father is a baronet. (For the benefit of any member of the middle-class this is like a knight in being 'Sir', but higher and also hereditary.) My only real fault is that my nose is a bit of a blob.

* * *

Hockey was off, because of the rain, so we went for a deeply dismal Set Walk among the trees and things. Miss Flower, whom we called Blossom, strode heartily along in her plastic hood exhorting us to breathe deeply. Janet walked with Melissa, and Mary-Rose with Virginia. I walked with a quite clever girl called Lavinia Beard, whom I patronise occasionally. We discussed poetry.

* * *

In the evening, after Prep, I wrote a rather good poem:

Poets in ancient chaos sang
Love, and the calling of the Gleam.
A million years can only hang
Variations on their theme.

Tonight you make familiar show:
'I love you thus, I love you thus—'
As they, a million years ago,
Made it in mockery of us.

In the first stirring of the sense,
Of sense and sensuality,
Am I to find my recompense,
Belov'd, for your banality?

And when you prize my lips, my eyes,
(Your murmurings grown moist with lust)
The poets that you plagiarise

Laugh through a million layers of dust.
But when your tongue transfixes mine,
Your touch electrocutes my breast,
My body sings the last-laugh line:
'They said it first—you do it best!'

I know this is at least one quatrain too long, but I can't decide which
to cut out. In point of fact I think each one so excellent that I can't
bear to cut any out. I realise this is an immature view.

'Belov'd' is perhaps weak, but 'My love' would get mixed up with
the 'my' in the previous line. And also the two B's are nice.

The other bit I feel uneasy about is 'My body sings', etc Possibly
the word for this phrase is 'mawkish'.

I will keep it, and improve it suddenly when I am twenty.

* * *

And of course the experience was imaginary. But I know all about that tongue thing when you kiss. And I know they do want to touch you down the front if you let them.

I touched mine after Lights, to see if I could feel what it would be like. But it was my own finger, and I could feel just as well from the finger as I could from the bosom, so it didn't convey anything. I made a mental note to try again, next time I woke up in the night with one of my arms gone completely to sleep from my lying on it. I would use this dead arm to see what a *foreign* finger felt like on my breast.

* * *

But when it happened a few nights later I was too sleepy, and didn't bother, and went back to sleep, and was livid with myself in the morning for missing the chance.

Chapter Two

The winter term has the Play. This year it was *Twelfth Night*. Miss Carrington, who is more sympathetic and perceptive than most of the staff, produced it. A girl called Diana Lowe was for some incomprehensible reason made Olivia, and Lydia Radcliffe was Viola. I was Maria. Maria is not a bad part, and it is true that I have an exceptional gift for comedy. All the same, I was definitely by far the best actress in the school, and it did seem a pointless waste not to give me the best part. This may sound like sour grapes, but really it is just realistic.

Virginia was Sir Andrew Aguecheek. She also has a promising gift for comedy, and is tall and thin. Melissa and Mary-Rose were sailors and Janet was an Attendant. The other people in it were mostly the usual dims and poops and wets you get at school.

Of course the Play gives the very small minority with real talent a certain scope, but its other great advantage is endless talking-time during rehearsals. The stage is quite grand – it is one end of the gym, and raised up, and has proper wings and things (somebody's father gave it quite recently), and underneath it has an endless dusty wooden rabbit-warren. It seems to be held up by tunnels. These tunnels were where we talked. Dukes and Captains and people would stump about overhead, trying to talk in blank verse, and Miss Carrington would tell them things, sounding very stagy and professional, and the stage would squeak and groan, and dust would flutter down, and we lay in the tunnels on bits of old costume and talked.

'I don't think I am capable of real love,' said Melissa.

'I used to think that,' said Mary-Rose.

'What changed your mind, Mary-Rose?' said Virginia.

'Love.'

'Your great lecherous blue-chinned bass?'

'God, no.'

'Another?'

'One of the others.'

'Straps keep slipping?'

'"What country, friends, is this?"' came Lydia Radcliffe's silly squeaky voice.

'"This is Iliyria, Lady."'

'Lady!' said Melissa. 'Hardly quite that.'

'It's not a question of shoulder-straps, Janet,' said Mary-Rose. 'It's something very much deeper and more spiritual, if you're capable of understanding the word. I am not just talking about something just purely grossly physical.'

'Impurely,' I said.

'Not physical?' said Melissa. 'Ah well, wake me up when you are talking about something physical.'

Mary-Rose shrugged (quite difficult when you are lying on your tummy).

'But if it wasn't shoulder-straps or something,' said Janet, 'how did you ever get started?'

'An immediate rapport.'

'You don't pronounce the T,' said Melissa. 'It's French. Rappor.'

'Rappor, then.'

'Yes, but what happened?' said Janet persistently.

'Aha.'

'It sounds a stinky wash-out to me,' said Melissa.

'Yes, it was,' admitted Mary-Rose. 'I thought he wanted to—'

'What? *Paw* you?'

'Yes, and so on. But I wasn't sure.'

'That's it,' said Virginia. 'The agony of not being sure.'

'Did you want to be pawed?' I asked austerely.

'Don't you ever, Sarah?'

'Certainly not,' I said. 'I know the pawing son. I demand a good deal more sophistication than that, thank you very much.'

But this was not really true. I didn't know the pawing sort. And I had longed quite often to be pawed. Respectfully, I mean, and sensitively and maturely.

'Virginia's right,' said Mary-Rose. 'If none of you were here, but *he* was—'

'Not blue-chin, but the other?'

'Yes, and we had this bit of Julius Caesar or whatever it is to lie on—'

'But you might still just sit and talk, easily,' said Melissa. 'That's what they do. They just sit and talk. They talk about cars.'

'Cricket.'

'Bell-ringing,' said Virginia feelingly.

'Pop.'

'Their families.'

'Their twelve-bores.'

'Twelve-bores themselves.'

'And you know why? Because they're not sure either.'

'But we can't tell them.'

'Mary-Rose can, with her shoulder-strap.'

'Stop going on and on about my shoulder-straps,' said Mary-Rose. 'I didn't mean to.'

'But that's what one needs. A symbolic shoulder-strap.'

'A signal. Something they understand.'

'A signal from them. Something you understand.'

'What?'

'What?'

'Like a particular colour buttonhole.'

'Ha ha, meaning "undo me".'

'A code-word.'

'What word?'

'Something Anglo-Saxon.'

'Scene 3, Scene 3,' came Miss Carrington's voice. 'Sir Toby! Maria!'

'Carrier-Bags calling,' said Melissa.

'Hell,' I said.

'Me too,' said Virginia. '*Merde.*'

'Nothing like a sign or a code-word,' said Mary-Rose thoughtfully. 'They just wouldn't work. There they'd be, but one still just wouldn't dare. You need ...'

'Maria! Sarah, dear, hurry up!'

'Come, sweet Sir Andrew,' I said to Virginia, 'list to Carry-Cot cooing.'

'Bless you, fair shrew.'

'You want it all fixed up beforehand,' said Janet. 'So just your being there is the signal. So you know straight away.'

'Divine,' said Melissa.

'Quite utterly totally imposs,' said Mary-Rose.

'Andiamo subito,' said Virginia.

It was funny, Janet being the one to have the absolute key central brilliant idea.

* * *

Virginia also brought this other book back the same term. (She stole them, really, from her parents, who were rather serious and cultured and very rich and bought a lot of books like that and never missed a few sexy ones.) This one was called *Prostitution – A Sociological Analysis.* It was interesting and boring at the same time. Mary-Rose and Melissa had awful arguments about it; Melissa saying that prostitutes were really wonderful and wise and the oldest profession, and Mary-Rose saying they were frigid and pathetic. They both always ended up saying: 'How do you *know?*' Naturally, Janet agreed with Melissa (which was even more ridiculous than usual, knowing Janet), and Virginia agreed with Mary-Rose. This went on most of the term (in the History Library and on walks and in the tunnels under the stage during rehearsals) along with other subjects, such as rape, day-versus-night for sex, Freud, Apartheid, Beethoven, Berry and Jonah, Whiteoaks, Lolita, suspender-belts, lesbianism, other people's crushes (which we thought deeply childish, and had grown out of), parents, incest, Tennessee Williams, culture, Debrett, different positions, and when we first would and what it would feel like.

One time we were in our cosy tunnel and Carry-Pants was stamping about over our heads, trying to tell Diana Lowe how to be gracious and elegant and like a Countess (which anybody could have told her was an utterly fruitless pointless foredoomed effort), and Janet made another interesting remark.

'*You* two—' she said, meaning Mary-Rose and Virginia – '*you* two say all prostitutes are all automatically invariably frigid.'

'They must be, don't you see,' said Virginia, 'or they couldn't bear to.'

'They couldn't bear to for money,' said Mary-Rose.

'All right, so you say. But supposing you could bear to, and in fact liked it, but happened to get paid?'

'Imposs,' said Mary-Rose.

'Jamais de la vie,' said Virginia.

'Why? Why is it?'

'Because,' said Virginia patiently, 'if you felt enough for a man to let him—'

'I could feel enough,' said Melissa throatily, 'for *any* man to let him do *anything,* after nearly a whole entire stinking creeping term in this dump.'

'Frustration,' said Mary-Rose.

'Yes!'

'That's exactly what I mean,' said Janet, like a terrier. 'We're all equally frustrated. Aren't you frustrated, Virginia?'

'God, yes.'

'Mary-Rose?'

'Moi aussi.'

'Sarah?'

'Frustrate Terrifico.'

'There you are. If somebody happened to pay, it wouldn't make any difference.'

'We're in a highly artificial situation,' said Mary-Rose. 'Prostitutes don't go to boarding-school.'

'The fact remains,' said Janet, 'we'd jump at it even if we were paid. We'd love it *and* be paid.'

'Sounds too good to be true,' said Melissa.

'Molto,' said Virginia.

'Dream of bliss.'

'Ludicrously imposs,' said Mary-Rose.

'"Here comes the Countess: now heaven walks on earth!"' boomed fat slob Jennifer Bostwicke above my head.

'Diana dear, try to walk on a little more gracefully on that cue—'

'Poor old Caraway-Seed. Uphill work.'

'I'm on in a sec,' said Virginia. 'Anyway, Janet, our sad and parlous state of deprivation only happens to the upper classes.'

'Yes, and so?'

'We might love it and be paid, but that doesn't apply to real prostitutes.'

'I'm not talking about real prostitutes,' said Janet. (This was the interesting remark.) 'I'm talking about us.'

* * *

A few days after this it didn't rain for a wonder, and we had a hockey match. I was in the second eleven, which was a very peculiar thing. I can run extremely fast, and have an outstandingly good eye and also a remarkable tactical sense. I admit most of the first eleven were nearly two years or anyway a year older than me. The fact remains I was beyond any shadow of doubt the best inside forward in the school, far better than either of the gawky, spotty, awful creepy suck-ups who were the insides in the first eleven. But they were friends of Cordelia Symington, who played centre-half and had a bosom like a bolster and was captain – and there it was.

I never discussed this with the others, because it would have sounded like jealousy even to them. It was not jealousy, but simply an objective view of what happens when you have sycophants and cliques. And of course we five despised games.

As it happens, Mary-Rose was in the first eleven, as a winger. I admit she is quite fast. I suppose she once smiled at Cordelia, who I suppose immediately developed an overpowering crush on her. She pretends not to care or be proud of it, but on match days she is a bit distant with all of us (even Virginia) and goes and talks to Cordelia. Mary-Rose is not very mature.

This second eleven match was away, at a place called Furlong Hall. It was their first eleven. We went in a bus for miles, and then just lost by 2–3. I played an outstanding game, not actually scoring but *actually* responsible for both our goals. I got quite muddy. We had baths there and a match tea, and had to talk to their team, who were rather middle class. Afterwards we came back in the bus, as it was getting dark. I was sitting with Melissa, who was left-half, and Virginia, who was linesman. We bagged the back, as we always did, and had a divine half-hour to talk.

'I feel languorous,' said Melissa, stretching. She looked as though she hadn't had a bath (but I knew she had), but I must say she didn't smell, which many people do.

'Voluptuous?' said Virginia.

'Feline.'

'Cruel?'

'Sinful.'

'Skinful,' I said.

'I am in the mood for love.'

'So am I in the mood for love,' said Virginia.

'So am I in the mood for love,' I said.

'*We* are all in the mood for love. Much good it does us'

'How does the driver strike you?' said Virginia.

'Male.'

'Ruthlessly male.'

'An enigma from here,' I said.

'It's dark, yes. And we can only see the back of his head, yes.'

'But one feels an emanation, does one not? A virile vibration?'

'Sans doute.'

'He would be a pig in a poke, though.'

'A boar-pig in a poke.'

'A boar-pig,' said Melissa, '*for* a poke.'

'Melissa!'

'Hee hee.'

'How utterly,' said Virginia, 'I would not require to inspect the candidate.'

'Assuming a certain standard,' I said.

'Naturellement.'

'"Not bus drivers.'

'Perhaps not bus drivers.'

'Yes,' said Melissa, 'bus drivers or taxi drivers or anyone.'

Really, Virginia and I both agreed.

'I will run away,' said Virginia after a bit, 'and go on the streets.'

'You'll be arrested, then. There is a new law.'

'Of course. Nowadays you work in a club. I will run away and work in a club. Or a comfortable brothel.'

'What a pity there isn't one here,' sighed Melissa. 'Here at school.'

'Where? Under the stage?'

'The History Library.'

'All over the place,' I said sleepily. 'Now here, now there.'

'One management, various premises.'

'A steady clientele.'

'Of a certain standard.'

'Naturellement.'

'I will talk to the Headmistress,' said Melissa. 'It's a gap in the curriculum.'

'I think you should. What part of education is more important than sex education?'

'None, none.'

'No, don't talk to the Headmistress,' I said. 'This is a case for private enterprise.'

'Will you be the Madame, Sarah?'

'I'll be the Madame,' I promised.

'I'll give exotic dances,' said Virginia, 'to excite the clients.'

'I'll be called Fifi,' said Melissa, 'and charge extra for certain specialised services.'

'Mary-Rose and Janet can do an *exhibition.*'

'What will you do, Sarah?'

'Yes, Sarah? What will you do?'

'Run the joint and take my commission,' I said.

Many a true word is spoken in jest.

* * *

A bit after this the Play took place. Various parents came, including mine. It was the very end of term, so they were staying a day or two in a reddish hotel near by and then driving me home. My father had a Bentley; Melissa's father had a Rolls, which is exactly the same thing only more ostentatious; Mary-Rose's had a 3.8 Jaguar; Virginia's had (and still has) a very old, huge Daimler, which I think is being ostentatious in the opposite – direction from Melissa's family. Poor Janet always went on a train to Scotland, where it was sad because her father only seemed to have a squadron of Land Rovers.

One of the ridiculous things about plays is that the actors with the biggest parts automatically get the most applause and take the most curtain-calls, even though very much finer performances are given by more talented people who happen to have smaller parts. The principals all tried hard and gave better performances than one might have expected. One is not a prima-donna.

Afterwards my mother said: 'You were marvellous, darling. You made us laugh like anything.'

'Thank you, Mummy,' I said modestly.

'Dear Virginia has a real gift, I think.'

I did not know if she meant a real gift *too,* or a real gift *as opposed.*

'She is promising,' I said.

'Mary-Rose looked sweet,' said my father.

'A walk-on part.'

'Yes. Pity, that.'

We were eating sausage-rolls and stuff at a sort of stagy party afterwards, for the cast and a few parents and Miss Carrington. I left my make-up on to remind them all. Virginia was talking French to a French aunt of hers like an Egyptian vulture. We wore dressing-gowns and things. Grease-paint has a most intoxicating smell.

'Darling,' said my mother, 'I was talking to Miss Abbott earlier this evening.'

Miss Abbott is the Headmistress. My heart sank.

'As a matter of fact, it was during the interval of the play.'

My mother always likes to give you the exact time and place in all her stories. She feels they will have more weight.

'We were standing,' she went on, '*very near* the door of the theatre.'

'The gym.'

'The gym. She says that you and Virginia and Janet and Mary-Rose—'

'And Melissa.'

'And dear Melissa, whose parents we know less well nowadays than we used to … She says you five—is it five?'

'It always was.'

'Exactly, darling. She feels you all might benefit from a wider circle of friends—'

'You don't know what's available.'

'There are any number of charming girls, darling. Only look at them all.'

'Charming,' said my father.

'You ought all five to mix more and take more part in free-time activities—'

'Madrigals? Embroidery? Poetry-reading? Botany?'

'*Yes.*'

'As a matter of fact,' I said, 'I think I am going to take up some very interesting free-time things next term, Mummy.'

'Oh good.'

'I have recently been reading a sociological analysis of various sociological problems.'

'Yes, darling?'

'Yes.'

'And will you do your sociology with other girls besides your own little set, Sarah? Promise?'

'Yes, Mummy, I think I can promise.'

'Them too, of course. I am not asking you to cut yourself off from your friends, you realise, darling.'

'They will certainly be involved.'

'Perfect, darling. I am so pleased.'

'Education,' said my father, 'is nothing if it's not preparation for life. You learn to meet, you learn to mix, you lead if you're a leader.'

'Exactly, Daddy.'

'Or so they used to tell me. Quite whether it applies to girls—'

'I am positive it does.'

'Yes. Have some more cocoa?'

'No, thank you.'

* * *

We said goodbye in the morning.

'Good hunting,' said Melissa.

'Foxes or males?'

'Foxy males.'

'Bristly, gingery males.'

'I expect I shall see *him* next week,' said Mary-Rose.

'And will you—?'

'Will he—?'

'It is in the womb of time.'

'I suffer and sigh for freedom.'

'For tenderness.'

'I shall have intrigues this Christmas.'

'I shall make some staggering New Year's resolutions.'

'Revelations,' I said, 'next term, then.'

'I shall resolve to be a much worse girl.'

'Wanton.'

'Animal.'

'Promiscuous.'

'It's funny, my blood gets gradually hotter every month.'

'You are blossoming into womanhood, dear.'

'I must go and catch my Jaguar taxi. Happy hols, chums.'

'See you next term, you plucky little winger.'

'The most popular girl in 5B tossed her golden bob and gripped her friend's hand.'

'Alas, her friend was holding some chewing-gum.'

'Goodbye, goodbye, goodbye.'

Chapter Three

During the Christmas holidays, only one event of importance happened.

Christmas came and went, and I was given various quite expensive presents. Just before dinner on Christmas Day I was drinking a glass of champagne, which is the only alcohol I can be bothered with, and I caught sight of myself in the big looking-glass in the drawing-room. (It is Chippendale, of course.) I was looking lovely My dress was dark-blue silk, very flattering, and my hair was shiny and sleek, and I could hardly see my glasses. (I may not have mentioned that I wear glasses.)

Boxing Day was warm and wet and like November. I felt a bit jaded and let down. Everybody went hunting, though not on horses except for my younger sister Annabel, but I spent the afternoon sitting on the bottom step but one of the kitchen stairs. I don't know why I sat there, but while there I wrote this rather good poem:

POEM IN NOVEMBER

Eachwhere rain has followed plough,
Earth is soaken brown.
All bewildered on the bough
The yellow leaves hang down.
Finch and wren forgetting nest,
Thrush and blackbird dumb:
God, that sinners pardonest,
God, that my love were come!

In a way this was a cheat because of course it was December when I wrote it. But I had a November feeling. I personally find that the archaic bits are effective and justified. I suppose it is all rather like 'When wilt thou blow, thou Western wind', but I think it is every bit as poignant and sincere. Perhaps this is not a mature view.

And of course when I wrote 'God, that my love were come!' what I truly meant was 'God, that *any* love were come!'

* * *

Funnily enough, five days later I thought he had. It was at a New Year's Eve party at a house belonging to some people called Myrtle. My father said I would be allowed to be grown up, which is laughable when to look at me you would quite often have said I was.

The Myrtles' house is all mushroom carpets and pale wood. It seems like the middle of London instead of the depths of the country, and not so much a house as part of Harrods. My father likes them because of Major Myrtle's shoot, and also they have racehorses and good tips and things. My mother says they are kind. I always sense something a bit sinful in the atmosphere there, so although it is so ugly I blossom and bloom.

I even took my glasses off that evening, as it is worth blundering a bit. *Il faut souffrir*, etc.

For this reason, when Colin asked me to dance, and I did, I thought he was a boy called Royston Porter who lives near us. But it was Colin. I dance extremely well, provided I have a partner who dances the same sort of steps I do (they taught us at school, not altogether badly), and luckily Colin did. We whizzed away in a waltz, and I only got to look at him properly at the end. He was at least seventeen and quite slim and elegant but strong. He had a nice voice, and he sang some of the words of the songs. He said he had been drinking whisky and soda, and could drive, and would be going into the army next autumn as an officer in the Horse Gunners.

'Why the Horse Gunners?' I said softly. 'I would rather go into the Brigade, but it would upset my father.'

'But the Horse Gunners have nice hats. They let off guns in the park.'

'You're thinking of the HAC.'

'Perhaps,' I said mysteriously. 'For me the army has a fascination.'

'Not for me.'

'What are you doing now, Colin?'

'Dancing with you, Sarah, I'm glad to say.' I felt weak and flowery.

'But at other times?'

'School.'

'*Still?* But you look far too mature.'

'I do, don't I? Many people ask if I am at Oxford.'

'What school?'

'Longcombe.'

'No! Then we are neighbours. I am at Bryant House.'

'I don't think I know Bryant House.'

'A bare twelve miles away, Colin.'

'Perhaps we shall see each other next term.'

'Perhaps,' I whispered.

We danced to one of the sad old tunes my parents sing while they are dancing. I wondered whether we might dance cheek to cheek, which I had never done but which looks so sophisticated. Several people were. But Colin did not pull me towards him, and it seemed awkward for me to crowd in. And his cheek looked a bit sweaty. So we swivelled about in the double drawing-room (the mushroom carpets were up, of course) and the party got noisier and noisier.

'Hullo, darling,' called my mother. 'Having a lovely time?'

'Yes, thank you,' I said demurely. 'Are you?' murmured Colin.

'Yes,' I breathed. 'You are lovely, you know.'

'Oh no.'

'Yes you are. Absolutely lovely. Let's go for a walk.' We stopped dancing suddenly. I felt throbby and confused 'You mean next term?'

'Now.'

'But it's cold.'

'Not indoors.'

I felt like giggling in a frightened way. 'We can't go for much of a walk indoors.'

'Yes we can. We can pretend we are going to get some food.'

'But I couldn't,' I said chokily, 'possibly eat.'

'It is only an excuse.' He began to speak very loudly. 'Let's go and have something to eat!'

'All right,' I shouted back.

So we walked out and along a passage and up some stairs and down some stairs and got to a little room with a chair and a desk.

'What is this room?' I muttered.

'It looks like—' Colin began, but his throat was hoarse and he had to cough. 'Sorry. An office thing, I suppose.'

'Shall I sit down?'

'No ...'

He took hold of my shoulders and began to kiss me, and I put my arms round his neck. Our noses bumped once, but we managed very well. He was panting, and this excited me. I hugged him. I felt his hand on my bosom, outside, and I nearly screamed with surprise for a second, but luckily I didn't. His hand felt very nervous, and I wondered how to encourage it, so I kissed him a bit. His hand took courage and presently tried to poke down inside. But the dress was tight at the front and cut ridiculously high, and we were standing close together so it was awkward for him. Then some footsteps clumped by and he shot away from me.

'It's all right,' I said in a funny voice.

'Somebody might come in.'

'No they won't.'

'They might easily.'

'I'm sorry you don't like kissing me.'

'I do, Sarah!'

'You don't seem to.'

'I swear I do! But we ought to be getting back to the party.'

I just said, 'Why?' I felt hurt and furious and terribly disappointed.

'It will look funny.'

'Perhaps.'

25

'We ought to get back.'

When it came to the point, I realised, it was the other way round from what you would expect. I was brave and he was frightened. I was eager and he was reluctant. This would be the case, nearly always: not, perhaps, when one got a good deal older, but certainly while one was young. This was a flash of intuition. I am often very perceptive. I could see it was an important lesson for the future.

We began to walk back along the passages, rather far apart.

'I'm sorry,' he said.

"What for?'

'Well ...' He looked very miserable, but so wet I couldn't feel sorry for him. In another flash of what I can only call inspired understanding I realised that men were contemptible.

'I expert,' I said, 'there are lots of boys like you at Longcombe.'

'Like me? In what way?'

'Lecherous but cowardly.'

'That's not quite fair.'

'Perhaps not,' I said, insincerely but diplomatically. 'I'm sorry if I sound rude. I mean I expect you are all very virile but frustrated.'

'God, yes. The maids are a wash-out.'

'Don't you have romantic feelings for smaller boys?'

'Where did you ever hear that?'

'I suppose I read it.'

'Only perverted swine go in for that sort of thing.'

I saw he had recovered his spirit, so I said, 'What you want is things arranged for you.'

'What things?'

'Assignations and things.'

'What on earth are you talking about?'

'I understand your problem perfectly. I think we can solve it.'

'What? What did you say?'

We had reached the edge of the party, and the noise was tremendous. No one saw us arrive.

'The Syndicate will arrange everything,' I said gravely.

'The what? I can't hear.'

'The Syndicate,' I shouted at him so that he could hear over the stereo thing. 'The Syndicate will meet your needs.'

I realised that I had our name and our slogan. The Syndicate. *The Syndicate Will Meet Your Needs.*

Almost at once it was midnight, and we drank toasts and sang, and people kissed one another.

With a courtesan gesture, I raised my glass to Colin.

'To fulfilment.'

'To what?'

'I will get in touch with you.'

'Darling,' said my mother, 'where have you been? Who is this, may I meet him? What have you been talking about?'

'Business,' I said quietly.

Chapter Four

Just before the beginning of term I went down to the estate office and borrowed the typewriter.

My father was working with the cow-man on the cow-book.

'What are you doing, Sarah? Writing a letter to *The Times?*'

'My sociology for next term, Daddy.'

'Aha. Do you know what sociology is?'

'Some aspects, yes.'

'More than I do,' said Parsons, the cow-man, with a fat and rather patronizing laugh.

My father laughed too, in a disloyal way. 'It's a wonderful thing, a modern education.'

If you make it so, I thought; and I began typing.

SECRET AND UTTERLY CONFIDENTIAL

THE SYNDICATE

Chairman:	Miss Sarah Callender
Members of the Inner Council:	Miss Virginia Goldsmith
	The Lady Janet Wigtoun
	Miss Mary-Rose Byng-Bentall
	The Hon. Melissa Bristow
Members of the Outer Division:	To be appointed

OBJECTS OF THE SYNDICATE

Whereas the female approaching maturity is denied male companionship by the modern upper-class educational system, thus being exposed to the dangers of perversion, introversion, and frustration;

And whereas, during our periodic opportunities for contact with the male sex, outworn and restrictive social conventions make it difficult if not impossible for true and fruitful relations to develop;

And whereas adolescent members of both sexes are conditioned by training and upbringing to a sterile and unnatural caution and reserve;

And whereas we know jolly well exactly the same applies to boys;

And whereas we can't go on like this.

It is hereby resolved that Selected Representatives of each sex shall meet in places appointed by The Syndicate, the meetings to be guaranteed free from interruption by whomsoever, for Purposes of mutual research and education.

Scale of charges: To be determined.

'The Syndicate Will Meet Your Needs.'

I pulled the paper efficiently out of the typewriter and read the document through to myself.

'Finished your sociology?' said my father. 'Hardly begun,' I said. 'May I see?'

'It is only some preliminary notes.'

'Perhaps I can help.'

'Well, I think it will be more valuable if we do it all by ourselves, you see. It will be more instructive.'

'Perhaps you're right. But if you want a hand let me know. I'm really quite well-informed, though you may not find that easy to believe.'

'I *know,* Daddy.' I tucked my document away in the pocket of my trousers. 'Really I ought to go and pack now.'

'All right, Professor.'

After I had gone out I heard them laughing again. Ho, I thought, little do you know.

* * *

'It's beautiful,' said Melissa a week later in the History Library.

'Your names are in no particular order,' I said. 'It's just the way I happened to type it.'

'What is the Outer Division?'

'Demand may exceed supply if it's only us,' I said.

'We can supply a good bit.'

'Yes, but my research indicates—'

'What research?'

'My preliminary market research. I carried out a pilot survey.'

'Goodness. Hark at the Chairman.'

'Somebody,' I said quickly, 'must be Chairman.'

'All right, we're not complaining.'

'I don't like "adolescent" much,' said Mary-Rose. 'It sounds babyish.'

'What about "sub-adult"?' said Virginia.

'Sub-normal, Sub-human.'

'Oh, all right. Near-adult?'

'I think that's a fair description of us.'

'"Near-adult,"' I said, clinching it. 'I'll make that change as the Inner Council directs.'

'The "whereas" bits are divine, Sarah,' said Mary-Rose, 'but—'

'Especially the last but one,' said Virginia.

'Especially the last,' said Jane

'But,' went on Mary-Rose, 'the *it-is-hereby-resolved* bit sounds utterly vague to me.'

'I couldn't spell it out,' I said.

'Yes you could,' said Melissa. She gurgled a bit. 'All those words are frightfully easy to spell.'

'I mean,' I said patiently, 'in a formal document of this kind, one naturally automatically chooses suitable language.'

'I suppose French would be the most suitable language.'

'D'accord,' said Virginia.

'What I mean,' said Mary-Rose, 'is, when you say "mutual research and education" what exactly is involved?'

'I imagine we all know what is involved,' I said stiffly.

'Don't get violent.'

'I am completely calm.'

'Ah well,' said Mary-Rose, 'all right. If you mean what it sounds as though you mean, that's all right. I just don't want to find myself being told things.'

'What is required is action, not words,' said Virginia.

'They speak louder,' said Melissa.

'Much louder.'

'Why not add that as a sort of additional slogan, Sarah? "Actions speak louder than words."'

'Yes, do, Sarah.'

'Is that the wish of the Inner Council?'

'*Nem. con.*'

'It is so resolved.'

'And when you put "selected representatives of each sex" in the same bit,' said Janet, 'how *many* representatives?'

'One of each, naturally,' I said.

'Ah, good.'

'We don't want Roman orgies, do we? Or do you?'

'No,' said Melissa. 'We want English orgies.'

'You shall have them,' I promised.

'Yum.'

'"*The Syndicate will meet your needs.*"'

'Hurray Actions speak louder than words.'

'Yum.'

'Shall we propose a vote of thanks to the Chairman?' said Virginia.

'Agreed, agreed.'

'Thank you,' I said, bowing.

'More soup, Sarah?'

'A drop.'

'So now what?'

'Now that we are agreed on the general policy of The Syndicate,' I said, 'we must negotiate with Longcombe.'

'Ah, Longcombe,' said Melissa.

'What else? Do you pine for a bus driver?'

'No, Longcombe will do nicely. The whole of Longcombe.'

'Less smelly than bus drivers,' said Mary-Rose.

'Better spoken.'

'Richer.'

'No,' I said, 'not so rich. But more respectful.'

'Agreed, agreed.'

'I have got my contacts alerted,' I said. 'Do I have the Inner Council's authority to proceed.'

'I think we should give the Chairman authority to proceed.'

'Do you want a secretary or anything, Sarah,' said Janet. 'An *assistant* Chairman?'

'Not at this stage.'

'But might you?'

'We shall see.'

'Can it be me?'

'We shall see.'

The bell went for classes and we all stood up.

'Bloody maths.'

'Attend to your maths,' I said. 'We shall need maths.'

'For what?'

'For money.'

'Money too. Yum,' said Melissa. 'I feel like Christmas all over again.'

'I feel like spring.'

'I feel like throbbing, teeming summer.'

'Hurry,' I said. 'Maths.'

* * *

That evening I wrote a business letter to Colin.

Dear Colin,

Further to our conversation on New Year's Eve. If you and the other Longcombes are still as frustrated as you said, The Syndicate is prepared to be of service to *selected clients.*

It is clearly understood that all payment will be *Cash in Advance.*

Please reply at your earliest convenience, and we will arrange a meeting place suitable to both, to discuss matters.

Half-way between would be best.

Awaiting the favour of your esteemed reply.

Love from,
SARAH (CALLENDER)

'*The Syndicate Will Meet Your Needs.*'
'*Actions Speak Louder Than Words.*'

I posted it on Tuesday afternoon, and nothing happened for days. The others kept saying 'Well?' Then on the following Monday morning, at breakfast, a ridiculous prefect gave me a blue envelope with a shield on the back and a tiny Latin motto.

'Well!' said Melissa, who sat next to me.

'My contact, I think.'

Colin's letter said:

Dear Sarah,

Thank you for your letter. I should say we are frustrated. And the term has hardly begun. What is the syndicate? Are you one of it?

We would pay in advance if you like, but not much, except for a few people who get colossal allowances.

Half-way between or a bit further towards you would be fine. I could bike.

Looking forward to seeing you,
Many thanks again.
Yours,
COLIN (SANDERSON)

I gave it to Melissa and she read it with a frown.

'He's got hopelessly unformed writing.'

'Yes, he is nothing special.'

'And he doesn't sound very keen.'

I remembered his hand in the little office place at the Myrtles'.

'He's keen all right. He's just cowardly.'

'Sounds divine, I don't think.'

'He'd be perfectly all right if he felt absolutely safe.'

'Does one ever?'

'But Melissa,' I pointed out softly, 'that is what The Syndicate is for.'

'Ah, yes. Gumdrops. When will you meet him?'

'Let's see—when can I? I shall want a whole afternoon.'

'No such thing in this joint.'

'It'll have to be at night, then.'

'Golly. Will he?'

'I don't know. Yes, of course he will. I'll have to write again. God, what a lot of time it wastes.'

Dear Colin,

Yours to hand. Do you know a Transport Cafe on the main Lingbourne road about two miles beyond the Horse and Hound? I mean two miles your side of it. Can you meet me there? They are discreet.

The best time would be about half past ten any night. Ring up here (tel. no. as above) and say you are my Uncle from Shropshire. Ring up between 7 and 8. Then we will fix the night. This meeting will be purely a business discussion.

Yours,

SARAH

'The Syndicate Will Meet Your Needs.'
'Actions Speak Louder Than Words.'

I showed this to the others before I sent it, and they were decently impressed with my planning. 'How will you get there?' asked Janet.

'Your bicycle.'

'OK.'

'Will you go alone?'

'No, I think one other person.'

'Why?'

'Security. Witness.'

'God. Who? Me?'

'Or shall we draw lots?'

'I trust you all equally,' I said. 'I suggest you draw lots.'

They drew lots with pencils, and it was Mary-Rose.

'Oh Mummy,' she said. 'How petrifying.'

'Be brave.'

'I'll try.'

'Sarah will be there.'

'Yes, that's comforting.'

* * *

Colin rang up three nights later.

'Hullo?'

'Hullo? Uncle Colin?'

'Aunt Sarah?'

'You're not alone?'

'No, are you?'

'No,' I said. I was in the little room off the Staff Common-Room, where we were allowed to take telephone calls. I had to be careful because I knew they could hear perfectly through the door and there were several odious mistresses sitting in the staff room correcting things.

'I got your letter,' said Colin.

'Yes? Is it all right?'

'Can't you manage an afternoon?'

'No.'

'It's a bit awkward. I've got to … make all kinds of arrangements, then.'

'Well, so have *I.*'

'Yes, I suppose so. All right. When? Tonight?'

'Yes,' I said eagerly 'No,' I added, feeling it was bad for business to sound too compliant.

'Tomorrow?'

'Yes.'

'Fine, then. Shall I come alone?'

'If you like, or bring one other. I shall bring one other.'

'I will too, then. Ellis, I expect.'

'See you there.'

'Goodbye. See you there.'

I emerged from the telephone room, and an old bag called Ex-Lax looked up from a lot of verbs.

'Sarah.'

'Yes, Miss Laxton?'

'Was that your uncle you were talking to?'

I felt a terrible blush go simmering up my face. 'Yes, Miss Laxton.'

She stared at me beadily through her little steel spectacles. I stood there palpitating, wondering if everything was going to be kiboshed before we even started.

'You did not speak to him very respectfully.'

'Oh.' I felt a wave of relief like a Cornish roller. 'He's a very young uncle. Really a cousin. Only about—well about—only about twenty-five.'

'Nevertheless, you should be polite. Especially on the telephone.'

'Why especially on the telephone, Miss Laxton?'

'Don't be impertinent, Sarah. Run back to your prep.'

I beamed at her maternally, poor old bag, and undulated out of the Staff Common-Room.

* * *

So the next night we set out, and it was horrid.

We bundled up our clothes before we went to bed, and crept out together at ten. Getting out was childishly easy, and we would have done it often if there had been anything to do once out.

36

Now there would be, I thought.

We dressed in the bicycle-shed, and then sped away towards our rendezvous.

'This is utterly loathsome,' said Mary-Rose.

'You didn't have to come.'

'I didn't mean that. Everyone accepts you as Chairman.'

'Anyway it's not raining.'

'Yet.'

We pedalled and pedalled, and got there ten minutes early.

'Got any dough?' I said.

'Yes, masses. Shall we scoff something while we wait?'

'Or do you suppose they'll wait outside and not dare come in?'

'If they're like that,' said Mary-Rose, 'we'd better find somebody else anyway.'

This was sensible of her. Mary-Rose may be quite useful, I thought.

So we went in and had greasy coffee and some ham-rolls. They were excellent after our revolting high tea. One or two lorry drivers were sitting quite still and silent over empty teacups. It was a dismal place, made of cardboard and tin-cans.

'So what is this Ellis?' said Mary-Rose.

'I don't know. Another witness.'

'He and I are seconds.'

'We're not *duelling.*'

'Almost. Bargaining.'

'Here they are.'

Colin was peering in through the dirty glass door. He saw us and pushed in. He was wearing about six sweaters and huge gloves and a great scarf; he looked overcome with heat prostration.

'We came like stink,' he said. 'Hullo, Sarah. I didn't know you wore glasses.'

'I wear them for bicycling at night,' I said. I took them off and put them on the table. 'This is Mary-Rose Byng-Bentall Colin Sanderson.'

'How do you do? This is Ellis.'

'Harold Ellis,' said Ellis, coming up behind Colin. I could not see him properly because of not having my glasses, but he seemed dark and stocky and about thirty.

'How do you do?' I said. 'Are you a *master?*'

Ellis laughed. 'I ought to be. What are you drinking? Coffee? Any beer in this dive, do you suppose?'

But they had coffee and ham-rolls too, and we all sat down and looked at each other.

'What now?' said Colin.

'I don't know,' I admitted.

'Good lord, you made us come all this way against a ghastly head-wind—'

'I mean, we discuss arrangements,' I said firmly.

'Are *you* the syndicate?' said Ellis suddenly, looking at us both in an appraising way.

'Yes,' said Mary-Rose, looking at Colin in an appraising way.

'We are here purely as spokesmen,' I said.

'The syndicate will meet your needs,' said Ellis. 'Is that right?'

'That is our slogan.'

'If it meets my needs it must be quite something.'

'What are your needs?' I said distantly. 'The usual, but more and oftener.'

'Ellis doesn't play games because of his asthma,' said Colin. 'So he hasn't got anything to work it all off on.'

'Goodness,' said Mary-Rose.

'The thing is,' said Ellis, 'do we have to come all the way to your school? Every time? And *back?*'

'It's only twelve miles.'

'Twenty-four.'

'We will try to make it worth your while.'

'Yes, but, *and pay?*'

'It is normal, I believe.'

'How much?'

'Yes,' said Colin, 'how much?'

We had discussed this at enormous length. Janet at one end of the scale had said two pounds; Melissa at the other end had said ten bob. (It was funny, having them on opposite sides in an argument.) We fixed on a pound. 'Thirty shillings,' I said. 'Good lord. Count me out.' 'Or near offer.'

'Fifteen bob,' said Ellis.

'A pound.'

'Seventeen-and-six.'

'No, a pound. It's very cheap, actually.'

'All right. I don't know where we shall raise the wind.'

'Shall we have some more coffee?' I said. 'And ham-rolls?' said Mary-Rose. 'That's right,' said Ellis. 'Feed up for the sacrifice.' One of the lorry drivers stumped out, and his mammoth lorry ground away. Colin went over to the counter to get another load of everything, and I went to help him.

He ordered, and then when the man went off to fiddle with the urn, turned to me. 'I say, Sarah—'

'Yes, Colin?'

'It is nice to see you again.'

'Thank you.'

'Really nice.'

Far from being the coward and wet I had briefly thought, I realised that he was actually very sweet, and respectful, and only needed confidence. Also he was very good-looking, especially now that he was not so overcome by his bicycling.

'It's nice to see you again, too,' I said.

'I don't expect you mean that.'

'Yes, I do,' I said truthfully.

'Look here,' he said. 'Listen—'

'Yes?'

'I don't like the idea of you being mixed up in this.'

'You're mixed up in it,' I pointed out.

'You know what I mean,' he insisted. 'People like Ellis, and so on … I should hate it,' he said, nervously but earnestly, 'if you *cheapened* yourself. I mean it would be horrible. I mean I don't mind about the others, in fact I'm glad, as you know, but not *you.*'

'That's all right,' I said. 'I'm just arranging things.'

'Oh good!'

'Of course, *I* wouldn't do anything like this.'

'Oh good,' said Colin. 'I am glad.'

As a matter of fact, I was not being altogether truthful: because I fully intended to cheapen myself terribly, and be dreadfully mixed up, and participate utterly. But one must be diplomatic with men. They do not understand. Colin might one day be adult enough to know the truth, but not yet.

Then our food and coffee came, and we carried it over to the others.

'At last,' said Ellis. 'Now listen—I take it you don't want ten-year-olds. You obviously want a guarantee of adequate, er—'

'Adequate maturity,' I suggested.

'Hey, here,' said Colin.

'Think of Squeaks Manson,' said Ellis. 'Waste of the syndicate's time.' He turned to us again. 'And you, on your side, of course, too—'

'We are in business,' I said coldly. 'So are we. Where do we start?'

We agreed that an unnamed client would arrive at the main gate of Bryant House on Friday evening at eleven. He would be met, and would pay a pound in advance. Then he would be guided to the assignation. We fixed a password.

'That seems to settle it,' said Ellis.

'You've got to guarantee this business of no possible interruption,' said Colin.

'We so guarantee.'

'And not just a bit of flowerbed,' said Ellis.

'What?'

'I mean, where will it be?'

'Adequate comforts are part of the syndicate service,' I said.

'One part,' said Mary-Rose.

Ellis laughed, and then paid for all our coffee and ham-rolls.

'Thank you very much. Who will come on Friday?'

'Someone with a quid.'

'He will be met.'

We went out and got our bicycles. It was pitch black and freezing and there was a howling wind.

'Goodbye,' said Mary-Rose, 'thank you for the coffee and stuff.'

'See you soon.'

'Ooh.'

They got on and whizzed away very fast. We wobbled out of the pull-in and rode away more slowly. We had the head-wind all the way back, and there was a bit of rain. We finally got to the dormitory and back into bed very late indeed.

'I hope I don't get Ellis,' whispered Mary-Rose.

'This is business,' I whispered back sternly. 'The Syndicate will meet your needs.'

She giggled. 'Actions speak louder than words. Happy dreams.'

Chapter Five

Bryant House is a large Georgian edifice standing in secluded parkland in quite nice country in a healthy pan of Southern England. Its former owners went broke, and it started being a school in about 1930. There can only have been six girls then, but now there are ninety, all paying rather high fees. They range from eleven to seventeen – mostly, of course, in the middle bracket of this range. The academic standard is unusually high, and the moral tone of the school is supposed to be high, too. The social tone is extremely high. All the girls and most of the mistresses live in the one vast building, which therefore has under its enormous leaded roof a prodigious quantity of repressed female emotion.

I thought about all this emotion as we crossed the stable yard from the labs at the beginning of break, the morning after our business meeting. We had been doing Biology. It must be awful for a spinster to teach Biology. Perhaps some of the younger mistresses could be included in the Outer Division one day. Perhaps they would entertain bachelor masters from Longcombe. But that was for the future.

'Time to draw lots,' said Melissa.

'History Library?'

'Come on.'

It was very solemn. We sat in the History Library and sipped cups of Chicken Noodle, and it felt almost sacramental, which I suppose is rather awful. We felt a more ritual form of drawing lots than usual would suit this historic occasion. Normally we drew pencils – the one that wasn't bust was it. After an argument we did it with books: five identical green ones called *England In The Middle Ages: An*

Introduction For Junior Forms. We put a bit of paper in one, well hidden in the middle, which said 'You!' Then we shuffled them around like playing-cards, on top of the History Library table.

'Junior Forms,' said Virginia. 'Is that what we've got? Junior Forms?'

Mary-Rose inhaled her breath and stuck out her bosom. 'I think some of us have got very nice senior forms.'

'Meet your needs,' murmured Melissa.

Janet giggled in a high, whiny way. I felt excited and frightened.

Finally we decided that the books were shuffled and we each took one.

I picked mine up very carefully, as though it were full of static electricity. I opened it. There didn't seem to be a bit of paper. I rifled through it quickly, and then held it upside down and shook it. No bit of paper. I felt numb. It was partly disappointment and partly relief, and a very dead, flat feeling.

The others all held their books upside-down and shook them. Nothing happened for ages.

'It must be one of us,' murmured Virginia.

'None of us,' said Mary-Rose.

Then a white thing fluttered out of Melissa's book and lay on the table saying 'You!'

'Ooh ...'

'Melissa!'

'Congratulations!'

'Are you pleased?'

'Yes, I think so,' said Melissa in a choky voice.

'You were very keen,' said Mary-Rose.

'I am, only—'

'Backing out?'

'No, of course not.'

'Of course she's not,' said Janet.

'Good,' I said coolly. But I still felt shaky and peculiar. We must work out a lot of details.'

'Free Walk this afternoon.'

Yes, we'll decide everything then.'

'I don't know if I'm thankful or disappointed,' said Virginia, voicing exactly my own thoughts.

'I do,' said Mary-Rose.

'Which?'

'Both at once.'

'Don't worry,' I said. 'Your turn will come.'

'Yes, of course.'

The bell went, and we put the fateful little green books away on the shelf. The piece of paper saying 'You!' stayed where it was, face up on the table. But just before Melissa went out, she picked it up and tucked it carefully away.

'Souvenir?' said Mary-Rose.

'Oh shut up.'

'Windy?'

'Not in the slightest, thank you very much.'

'Come on,' I said. 'Scripture calleth.'

'Here come the women of Babylon,' said Virginia. 'After you, Delilah.'

'Oh, shut up,' said Melissa.

She was a bit silent for the rest of the day.

* * *

On the Free Walk we went to a place off by itself near a dripping wood where three sad haystacks stood in a field. There was a large, a medium-sized, and a small haystack, and we called them the Three Bears. We always sat under Mother Bear, which may have been a bit psychological.

'This will be a wonderful place in the summer,' said Virginia.

'What for?'

'Us. Them.'

'The Syndicate?'

'Meeting needs.'

'These haystacks?'

'Our dear Bears.'

'Prickly.'

'We'll have rugs and things. Hay is very sexy stuff.'

'Not for poor Ellis,' said Mary-Rose, 'with his asthma.'

'I wonder who will appear tomorrow night,' said Janet. 'You must be wondering, Melissa.'

'Yes,' said Melissa shortly.

He will have bicycled a long way. Will he be exhausted?'

'Oh God,' said Melissa.

'What will you wear?'

'It doesn't matter, does it?'

'But it does. You must wear something slinky and provocative.'

'Rot.'

'Well,' said Virginia, 'remember what it said in *Prostitution – A Sociological Analysis.* They always wear sexy clothes. It's half the battle.'

'That's a comfort,' said Melissa. 'Battle.'

'It's only an expression, dear.'

'That's another thing,' said Janet. 'Will he call you dear? Or what?'

'Darling?' suggested Mary-Rose.

'Tootums-Wootums?' said Virginia.

'Oh for God's sake,' said Melissa.

'Please all be quiet,' I said. 'We've got a lot of business to discuss.'

'Sorry, Boss.'

'It's all very well for all of you,' said Melissa. 'I'm the bloody guinea-pig.'

'I think it must be very alarming, being first,' I said gently. A true leader is always deeply concerned with the morale of subordinates.

'Not *alarming*,' said Melissa crossly. 'I'm not *alarmed,* good heavens, why should I be? You just all jabber about it so much.'

'We won't now,' I said. 'We'll discuss business details.'

So very efficiently we fixed times and places and duties, and splashed back to tea in a January drizzle.

* * *

45

The next afternoon was the afternoon of The Night, Janet and I slunk into the gym and piled a mass of old costumes and drapes and things in the best tunnel under the stage. When we had formed all we could find and drag into a huge double bed Janet flopped down on to it.

'Nice?' I said.

'Very comfortable.'

'Does it make you feel amorous?'

'Ye-es. It's a bit dusty.'

'They can't expect four-posters for a pound.'

'What are they going to do for light?'

'Torches.'

'What a waste of the batteries.'

'I expect they'll switch them off after a bit.'

'I suppose so. Sarah—'

'Yes?'

'Do you wish it was you and not Melissa?'

'I'm not sure. If it was me I should feel wildly excited, but—'

'But?'

'But I'd have rather a fear-of-the-unknown thing.'

'I wouldn't.'

'Are you sure, Janet?'

'Yes,' said Janet positively. 'I wish it was me. I'm dying for it to be me.'

'I didn't realise.'

'Neither did I.'

* * *

At eleven o'clock I was waiting by the main gates.

It was a dark night, but not absolutely pitch. I could see the great bulk of the main school building, a hundred yards away, with no lights on on my side. The headmistress's house (once a lodge) still had a light on. I imagined her reading sixth-form essays, wrapped up virginally in a Jaeger dressing-gown and drinking unsweetened cocoa.

I was also wrapped up virginally, but in a different way. I had on my old corduroy trousers, and three sweaters, and a headscarf I only wore at night with words saying 'Cheers' in different languages.

There was a breeze which made the bare trees whisper and chatter, but it was dry. There had been rain, and the drive was seamed with great khaki puddles. We should have to avoid these when the Client arrived and I guided him to the bower of love.

Everything had gone smoothly. Melissa was under the stage, in the big central tunnel, reclining on the softer remnants of *Twelfth Night*. She had Mary-Rose's torch, with a bit of yellow Cellophane over the glass, to shed a romantic glow. Virginia was stationed at the entrance of the tunnel, as an inner guard. Mary-Rose was at the main door of the gym and Janet at the side door. They were outer guards.

We had crept out with no trouble at all, and all dressed together in a giggly shivery way in the bicycle-shed. Like me, Janet and Virginia and Mary-Rose wore practical clothes. We had argued a lot about Melissa's garb. In the end she had put on a semi-evening dress and medium heels. As far as we could tell in the bicycle-shed, by the light of Janet's bicycle lamp, she looked very nice. Scent had been a problem. We knew (from Virginia's prostitution book) that scent was a thing the better class of *filles-de-joie* relied on a good deal to arouse clients. None of us had any. But a girl called Miranda Cave had some very sexy Italian soap, so we pinched that out of her bedside cupboard and wetted it and rubbed it on Melissa's arms and the back of her neck and behind her ears and down her front. She smelt marvellous just after we did it, but definitely soapy. We hoped the soapy smell would wear off and the sexy scent stay, but in fact, in the bicycle-shed, it seemed to me to be the other way round. I did not say this, because of Melissa's morale. At least The Client would know she was clean.

I waited and waited by the main gate, becoming gradually certain The Client wasn't coming. Perhaps nobody at Longcombe had a pound. Perhaps the Client had set off but had been run over or perhaps they had dismissed the whole thing as girlish prattle I grew gloomy, and rather frightened, and my feet got bitterly cold. I imagined the others waiting: Mary-Rose and Janet patrolling the gravel paths outside the gym, with shrubs rustling at them out of the darkness; Virginia in the great vault of the gym; and of course Melissa, sitting patiently on a mauve robe, waiting in a yellow torch-beam for her demon lover.

The minutes ground by like leisurely millstones, and I did a few jumps to keep alive.

The night seemed to grow blacker and blacker. The wind rustled about like a prowling mistress. Footsteps crunched all round me, and I got less and less able to be sure they weren't footsteps.

Suddenly there was a violent explosion of gravel immediately beside me, and I gave a small scream.

'Sorry,' said a polite black shape of enormous height.

'Oh,' I said, 'I didn't see you.'

'It's dark.'

'Yes. Haven't you got any lights?'

'I turned them off when I got near. Ellis told me to so as not to be seen.'

'Yes.'

'You are, er, The Syndicate?'

'Yes. Hey, what's the password?'

'Oh of course. Er, "I love my love with a P—"'

'"Because she is professional,"' I said crisply.

It was all right. He was bona fide.

'I'll guide you now,' I said.

'I've got this—'

'What?'

'This.'

He seemed embarrassed. Something crackled. I felt a piece of folded paper in my hand.

'Ooh,' I said. 'Is this a pound?'

'Yes.'

'Not ten bob?'

'Of course not.'

'No, of course, sorry. Come on then.'

'Where shall I leave this bike?'

'Shove it against the wall behind that bush. Come on, she's waiting.'

The tall dark shape seemed to twitch a bit.

'Suppose I can't find my bike again?'

'We'll remember. Look, just by the gates.'

'But it's Ellis's.'

'The Syndicate will guarantee to find it again.'

'Oh, all right.' He pushed it behind the bush, and then cleared his throat. 'All right. Well. Lead on.'

'Follow me,' I said.

I sploshed along the gravel, avoiding the puddles when I could, but stepping into a good many. I could hear crunching and splashing behind me and rather unhappy noises.

'What's the matter?'

'I've got my feet wet.'

'You can dry them when we get there.'

'Will there be a towel? But my socks are wet. Is there a towel there?'

'A velvet towel,' I said, remembering the mauve robe.

Really it was a kind of velveteen, about seven shillings a yard otherwise they never would have bought it for *Twelfth Night.*

'Velvet doesn't dry very well,' said the Client. 'Come on,' I said.

'Haven't you got a torch?' he said querulously. 'Not yet,' I said. 'Security.'

The dark mass of the gym gloomed up in front of us, and a shadow appeared and whispered 'Who goes there?'

'P1 and Client,' I whispered.

'Pass, P1 and Client,' whispered Mary-Rose.

'Thank you, P2.'

We went into the gym, and at last I got my torch out of my pocket. 'Here we are, safe,' I said.

'But you said it would be comfortable. Ellis said you said it would be comfortable.'

'Comfort is guaranteed. This is only the antechamber. I shone my torch at him. He looked respectable enough: very tall, with muddy grey flannel trousers and a tweed coat and a scarf and floppy gloves. He could be forgiven the mud; it would all be better when the weather grew warm and suggestive. His hair was a bit untidy, of course, but he couldn't help that after all his bicycling.

He blinked at the torchlight, and looked rather sweet, like a tall, embarrassed rabbit.

'OK,' I said. 'This way, sir.'

We climbed round to the back of the stage, and another shadow popped out from the wings and said, 'Who goes there?'

'P1 and Client.'

'Pass, P1 and Client,' said Virginia.

'Thank you, P4.'

Virginia and I lifted a bit of matting we had hung over the entrance to the tunnel. The golden light from Melissa's torch shone dimly out. 'Ooh ...' said Melissa's voice.

'Client has arrived, P5.'

'Ooh.'

'Proceed,' I said to the Client.

'In *there?*'

'You will be perfectly comfortable, and guaranteed safe from interruption. P5 is waiting. Mind your head.'

He crawled in, and we dropped the matting back over the entrance.

'What do we do now?' whispered Virginia. 'Go to bed, or what?'

'Guard.'

'Can I listen?'

'Quite unethical. Would *you* like it?'

'No. But I long to know.'

'You mustn't, Virginia. But guard like anything. I'll go and check on the outer defences.'

'All right.'

I found Janet by the side door and we challenged each other.

'So he's arrived?' said Janet.

'Safe and sound and a bit damp about the feet.'

'Melissa ought to dry them with her hair.'

'Yes. I wonder if she's thought of that?'

'I expect she's got other things to think about. Oh God,' said Janet, 'I wish it was me.'

'Your turn will come. Guard like mad.'

'Can't I come and listen?'

'You all want to listen,' I said severely. 'It's disgusting. Certainly not, Janet.'

'Well, Melissa will tell us.'

'God, yes,' I said. 'She'd better.'

Then I went and checked up on Mary-Rose. She said she was cold and wanted to go to bed.

'If you were Melissa,' I said shrewdly, 'you'd be glad to know the sentries were out.'

'But I'm me and my feet are falling off and I'm sleepy.'

'Your turn will come.'

'Must we all guard every time? We'll get dreadfully tired, and not be any good when our time does come.'

'But—'

'It says so in that book. And I've heard it from people. It's no good at all when you're tired. You don't respond.'

'We must respond,' I admitted.

'Us responding is the whole point.'

'Yes …' I could see (because I am not an unreasonable leader) that Mary-Rose had a point. 'Next time we might leave just two guards on.'

'And the rest go to bed.'

'We'll do it in rotation.'

'That will be much cosier. But I must say,' said Mary-Rose, 'I couldn't sleep till I heard Melissa's report. Not tonight.'

'Our first night.'

'Do you wish it was you, Sarah?'

'Yes,' I said, not quite truthfully.

'So do I, I think.'

'You were a bit bloody to Melissa.'

'I envied her, I think. And also it's become a habit, rather. It's silly, isn't it?'

'Well, guard like mad.'

'Or rather,' said Mary-Rose, still following her train of thought, 'it isn't so much that I envy her what she's doing now. It's more that I *shall* envy what she *will have* done. Aren't those tenses elegant? I *will* envy what she *shall have* done.'

'No, the other way was better. And do guard.'

'I will. And another time you will guard me. Two of you.'

'Yes, like mad.'

'Don't let Melissa tell till I'm there.'

'She must tell us all together.'

'The whole Syndicate.'

'The Inner Council.'

'OK, Boss. P2 signing off.'

'Roger. Over and out.'

'That's American. The English is just "out".'

'Just "out", then.'

I went back to Virginia's post and we sat and waited in the dark for a long, long time.

* * *

At last there was a rustle of matting and a pale glow of light from Melissa's torch. 'Shh!' I hissed.

'I wasn't saying anything,' whispered Virginia.

'Client.'

'Yes, I can see.'

I shone my torch at the tunnel entrance and The Client crawled out. He looked at us and we looked at him. His hair was more untidy than before, and he was putting his scarf back on. After a time he cleared his throat.

'I'll be getting back, then,' he said.

'I'll guide you to your bicycle,' I said.

'No thanks, I can find it.'

'All part of the syndicate service.'

'I'd rather find it by myself.'

'We do undertake to guide you—'

'I'd rather. Well—' he cleared his throat again – 'goodbye.'

'Goodbye,' said Virginia politely.

He squeaked out of the gym and vanished.

'Funny,' said Virginia.

'He seemed a bit—'

'Disturbed?'

'Tempest-tossed?'

'All passion spent?'

'Let's hope so,' I said.

I went to the tunnel entrance, and I was about to call Melissa when she crawled towards me.

'Well?' I said.

Melissa stumbled out and stood up. She looked a bit dishevelled.

'I expect my hair's a mess,' she said vaguely, pushing at it with one hand. She was right. It was a mess.

Mary-Rose came up.

'What an odd Client,' she said.

'Why?'

'He came past me and I said "Hullo" and he said "Hullo" and I said I hoped he'd have a nice ride back to Longcombe and he just coughed and raced away.'

'Overwhelmed,' said Virginia.

'They often are, I believe,' I said. 'All wordless and gaga. Well done, Melissa.'

'Oh,' she said modestly, 'it was nothing much.'

'So was it bliss?'

'God, yes.'

Then Janet came up.

'*Well?*' she said. 'Melissa?'

'Yes,' said Mary-Rose, 'so, come on, what happened?'

'What did he say first?'

'What did he call you?'

'Where did he start?'

'At the top?'

'Or the bottom?'

'Or half-way?'

'What did you feel like?'

'What did *it* feel like?'

'Was it divine?'

'Or disappointing?'

'Did it hurt?'

'And now you're different,' said Virginia solemnly. 'Different from us.'

'Yes,' said Melissa finally, in a throaty way.

'So was it bliss?'

'God, yes.'

'Tell!'

'Later. In bed.'

'Now. Please. Please.'

'Please, Melissa.'

'Later,' said Melissa, sighing. 'I must recover a little first. You can't of course, quite understand—'

'God. You are different.'

'Yes.'

'I wish it was me,' said Janet.

'Let's go to *bed*,' said Mary-Rose, 'and then Melissa will tell.'

So we undressed again in the bicycle-shed and bundled up our clothes and crept back. Melissa got into bed, and the springs squeaked and she huddled down looking a bit shivery.

'Well?' I whispered authoritatively.

Then Melissa burst into tears and pulled the sheet over her head.

The rest of us looked at each other.

Janet sighed. 'Tomorrow.'

'Break.'

'History Library.'

'She's overwrought.'

'No wonder.'

'It must be a terrific thing, really,' said Virginia.

'An Experience.'

'But we'll know tomorrow.'

'I wish,' said Janet, 'I wish it was me.'

Chapter Six

'Well?'

'Well?'

'Well?'

'Well?'

'Well,' said Melissa. She was staring at her slowly-revolving, mud-coloured, faintly-steaming packaged chicken broth-avoiding our eves. 'As a matter of fact it was a wash-out.'

'Not total?'

'Total. Utter.'

'Oh God.'

'I didn't want to be first.'

'I'm sure it wasn't your fault,' I said gently. 'Just tell us, and we'll know for next time.'

'I very much doubt if there'll be a next time. He'll tell Ellis and Ellis will tell the others and that's the end of The Syndicate.'

'Melissa—just tell us.'

'Tell you what? Nothing happened.'

'Something must have. I mean, negatively. So what did?'

'The same old trouble.'

'You mean, not knowing?'

'Not knowing.'

'You mean, not being sure?'

'Not being sure.'

'Oh, Melissa.'

'Don't say "Oh, Melissa."'

'Well,' I said, 'he scuttled into the tunnel—didn't he, Virginia?—panting with eagerness and so on—'

'Yes. And I was sitting there.'

'Yes. And he—what?'

'He said "Hullo." And I said "Hullo." And he said, "Well, how do you do?" And I said "How do you do?" And he cleared his throat a few times and then crawled along to the bed thing.'

'Good.'

'Good? He said "May I join you?" and I said "Please sit down," and he did.'

'Good.'

'Then he told me his name, and I told him my name, and he told me what form he was in, and I told him what form I was in, and we talked about games for a bit. Then he cleared his throat like mad and sort of scuttled his arm round my shoulder.'

'Yes, good.'

'So I thought. At last, I thought, this is what I've been waiting for. And so I was all excited and frightened and … you know!'

'We know. Poor Melissa.'

'Yes. Well. He was quite sweet, you see.'

'That's what we thought,' said Virginia. 'But a bit wet, we thought.'

'Oh God'

'But there his arm was …?'

'Yes. So then he began to talk terribly quickly about his exams and things. He is dreading the Latin unseens.'

'Oh no.'

'So I tried wriggling nearer and I tried getting further under his arm and I tried soulful amorous looks.'

'No good?'

'He just talked faster and faster. French unseens, he got to.'

'Poor Melissa …'

'Every so often he stopped. Dead. And coughed a bit. And seemed on the point of doing something—'

'Like what?'

'Like what I thought we were there for. But no. He always took a huge deep breath and gabbled on about the prefects.'

'Oh Melissa. What did you do?'

'In the end I said "Shall I switch the torch out?" And his arm shot away from my shoulder and he gabbled even harder about prefects. So I lost even the bit I had. So finally I got desperate.'

'Undo something? Buttons? Zip?'

'No. I just said, veil—'

'Well?'

'Well, I said, "Aren't you going to kiss me, or—anything?" And he looked at me in a terrified way and said, "Do you think I ought to?" And I said, "Just as you like." And he said "Not a bit."'

'And did he?'

'He made a sort of wild grab and I think he Kissed my hair, and then he bolted away.'

We all looked at Melissa with horror 'Poor Melissa,' murmured Mary-Rose. 'How ghastly.'

'I should have taken action,' said Janet. 'It's extremely ludicrously easy to say that now.'

'But I should.'

'All right,' said Melissa, 'next time you do.'

'I will.'

'You do.'

'The trouble—' said Virginia – 'of course the trouble was him being so embarrassed.'

'I suppose we both were.'

'Him more, though?'

'I suppose so.'

'How can we make it so they're not? Sarah, how *can* we?'

'Melissa, surely—when he *first* crawled in, an absolute stranger—anything could have happened?'

'I thought so.'

'But you did how-do-you-dos and names and normal conversation and things—and so by then it was like a tea-party. So of course it was embarrassing to start. So of course he didn't start.'

'I suppose so.'

'You're absolutely right, Mary-Rose,' I said. 'I see it all.'

'Blaming me,' said Melissa.

'No,' I said, 'it wasn't you. No one can blame you, Melissa The thing to do is to keep it like that first moment.'

'Aha,' said Mary-Rose. 'Yes. Two utter strangers.'

'No how-do-you-dos.'

'No names.'

'No forms and prefects and Latin unseens.'

'No faces?'

'Perhaps even masks, yes.'

'They'll be A3 or something.'

'We'll be Fifi or something.'

'Much darker,' said Melissa, at last coming to life a bit.

'Probably.'

'We've got to be professional,' I said.

'I'm sorry I was so amateur,' said Melissa.

'You've been a terrific help,' I said. 'Without your experience we'd all make the same mistake again.'

'Hear hear,' said Mary-Rose kindly.

'D'accord,' said Virginia.

'The Syndicate had better take the initiative,' I said. 'I'll write to Ellis.'

* * *

In the evening I wrote Ellis a letter.

Dear Mr Ellis,

The first Client sent by you to our Mlle Yvette was, according to Mlle Yvette's account, impotent or ignorant or both. Please ensure that future Clients you send do something. It is no good sitting for endless hours talking about French verbs. Mlle Yvette was bored and puzzled. Her feelings were hurt. She was happy and anxious to meet The Client's needs (see our slogan). But The Client seemed not to have any needs.

The Syndicate understands, though, that many Clients will be coming new to *services* of the kind The Syndicate provides. They may be shy and embarrassed. So we suggest as follows:

1. Darker and more mysterious premises will be provided. So they won't be quite so much meeting our Mlles as if it was a tea-party.

2. Names will not be used. Clients can introduce themselves by code-letters which you and we can fix. Our Operatives of course will use their professional names.

3. What do you think about masks?

Assuring you of our best service at all times, We are,
S. CALLENDER

'The Syndicate Will Meet Your Needs.'
'Actions Speak Louder Than Words.'

I posted this masterly missive in the morning, and then by the afternoon post a letter came from Ellis which must have crossed mine.

Dear Syndicate,
My friend reports total lack of co-operation by your person. I suggest a refund. You have to do better than this for £1 let alone the 24 miles.
Yours very sincerely,
HAROLD ELLIS

So I wrote immediately:

Dear Mr Ellis,
Yours to hand. There is no question of refunding the pound. Mlle Yvette was completely entirely ready and willing. Ladies do not

make the first advances, even Professionals. We are not Lolitas. Please say what you think about our suggestions.

Awaiting your esteemed reply, Yours very sincerely,

S. CALLENDER

'The Syndicate Will Meet Your Needs.'
'Actions Speak Louder Than Words.'

The upshot was that we went to the Transport Cafe again two nights later. This time I took Virginia, and the ride was beastly. Ellis and another boy were there already: Ellis looking squatter and darker and more Welsh than ever, and the other fattish and fair and financial-looking.

I took my glasses off and said 'Good evening. This is Mademoiselle Chantal.'

'Good evening. I am XI and this is K2.'

'How do you do?' said Virginia. 'But K2 is Italian cleaning stuff.'

'It can't be.'

'Yes, like Dabitoff, but a paste.'

'Then I will be K3.'

'But that is a mountain,' I said.

'No, K2 is the mountain.'

'I would rather be a mountain than Dabitoff,' said K3.

'Hurry up and sit down,' said Ellis. 'And it's your turn to buy the coffee.'

I went and got coffee and ham-rolls for four. K3 came and helped me carry it, which seemed out of character, but not as out of character as it would have been if Ellis had done it. When we got back, Virginia and Ellis were talking guardedly.

'Business,' said Ellis. 'What a time you've been.'

'No refund,' I said.

'No.' Ellis agreed. 'Hobson wanted one—'

'Hobson?'

'I mean The Client who came. So I tried it on. I thought he was a drip, but I didn't realise he wouldn't make a pass at all.'

'Exactly.'

'He said he was embarrassed.'

'So we gathered,' said Virginia.

'And that's why The Syndicate suggests a much more anonymous sort of thing,' I said quickly.

'I think you're right,' said Ellis. (In spite of looking so awful and having bad manners, he was reasonable. One could do business with Ellis.) 'Of course it wouldn't have bothered me, but I couldn't raise a quid.'

'Or me,' said K3, 'but Flobson won the raffle.'

'You *raffled* Mademoiselle Yvette?' I said, shocked.

'Well,' said Virginia, 'we drew lots.'

'Masks,' said Ellis, 'we thought not, as you're making it darker.'

'Agreed,' I said.

'Clothes, now.'

'Mademoiselle Yvette was extremely fashionably dressed.'

'That was Flobson's trouble, part of it. He didn't know what to do.'

'Mademoiselle Yvette would have done what was necessary.'

'But Flobson didn't know where to start. Or ask her. But if she'd been in a dressing-gown, even he—'

'Really!'

'It's normal,' said K3. 'Look at all those paperback covers. And in the films and things. They all do. Or else nothing but a mink coat.'

'Mink coats are not part of the syndicate service. Yet.'

'Then a dressing-gown. And then the chap knows where he is. And then even someone like Flobson—'

'All right.' I agreed, because I could see that it was sensible really.

We drank our coffee and fixed a new appointment and a password and so on. Then we bicycled away, full of hope.

* * *

We drew lots with the green books. Melissa, of course, was out of it. Virginia won. She began immediately to worry about dressing-gowns. We agreed to look for the most glamorous available, and borrow it.

61

The rest of us drew lots for the sentry jobs; it was Melissa and me, but Mary-Rose and Janet decided to stay on duty too, for at least one more time.

'To be in at the death,' said Janet.

'Thanks,' said Virginia coldly.

* * *

Yet again everything went perfectly smoothly on The Night.

(The discipline at school was not so much lax as unenforced. They thought they were strict, but they were bad at making sure. It was an extremely expensive school.)

Virginia was in the tunnel, in a quilted dressing-gown belonging to a girl called Anne Mostyn. Underneath that she had on pyjamas and under them (she insisted, and wouldn't be budged) woolly knickers. The sexy soap we had used to make Melissa provocative had obviously done nothing for her, so we used a bit of the first pound to buy some scent from a horrid, bald old woman in a horrid little shop. (Another furtive expedition.) The scent was called 'Jungle Venom' and smelt common but penetratingly sexy. Better than soap. And it gave Virginia confidence The dim mysterious amorous non-embarrassing light was easy, of course: we put some red Cellophane over the yellow Cellophane over the glass of the torch, and shone the torch against die wall of the tunnel instead of outwards over the bed. To me it all looked almost frighteningly right. One imagined orgies.

I was again at the gate, to take the money. But this time I *was* braver. The violent arrival of the new Client's bicycle hardly discomposed me, and I said 'Good evening, sir.'

'Q5,' he replied, panting, but thank God he didn't clear his throat.

'Password?'

'"I love my love with a W—"'

'"Because she is Willing." Right. One pound, please.'

'Here.'

It was all small silver.

'I shall have to check this,' I said.

'It's quite correct, unless I've dropped some.'

'One must be businesslike. Very well, follow me.'

Melissa challenged us by the door of the gym and Janet by the entrance to the tunnel. We lifted the matting.

'Mademoiselle Chantal is waiting,' I said.

The Client went 'Hmm!' and dashed in.

Janet and I checked the money by the light of my torch. It was exactly a pound. Then the others joined us, and we settled down to wait in the enormous whispering blackness of the gym.

* * *

The Client emerged distraught. He stared about him wildly, blinking in the beam of our torch. He was panting.

'There you are, then,' I said awkwardly, as something had to be said I must have sounded like a nanny.

He cleared his throat, which was a thing I had hoped this one didn't do. (But of course it was January, and he may have had a slight cold.) 'I'm not sure—' he said. 'I didn't realise ... I don't think it's what I meant ...'

'Complaint?' I said coldly. 'Mademoiselle Chantal did not please you?'

'No no,' he said hoarsely, 'no, no, no. I mean she did. I ... Will you tell her I'm sorry?'

'Did you hurt her? What? Or what?'

'What is all this?' said Janet.

'Oh no, no, no.' The Client gasped. He was gingery and curly and quite nearly going into the army, one would have supposed. 'Well, goodnight.'

He hurried off, and once again we all looked at one another. Then Virginia emerged. 'Your Client seemed in a state,' said Janet. 'Upset about something,' said Melissa. 'Surely not Melissa's trouble?' said Mary-Rose. 'Or was it?' said Melissa, obviously hoping it was. 'A bit different,' said Virginia slowly. She looked cool, but as though she had been uncool. 'Well?'

'Shall I tell you it all now? Or as we go back? Or tomorrow?'

'Now.'

'It's not very homey here in the dark.'

'Yes it is.'

'If you prefer, we'll go into your chambre d'amour,' said Mary-Rose.

'No thanks. It's a very nice chambre, but I don't want any more of it just now.'

'Then here.'

'All right. So. The light was right, because we could see what we were doing, but we couldn't see each others' faces properly. So it wasn't embarrassing in *that* way.'

'Good,' I said.

'Yes. And the scent was right, I think.'

'Three cheers for Jungle Venom,' said Mary-Rose. 'And the Yvette-Q5 business was right. So we didn't have a starting point for an ordinary conversation. So we didn't have any ordinary conversation. In fact we hardly talked at all.'

'Oh the bliss,' said Melissa.

'Though actually his voice was quite nice. So was his curly hair,' said Virginia.

'The Professional,' said Janet, 'never gets emotionally involved.'

'I am not emotionally involved, thank you very much. I am merely stating a fact.'

'All right, all right.'

'His hair happens, as a point of pure objective actual fact, to be curly I happen to mention this. Any objections?'

'No. Go on.'

'Thank you very much. Anyway, the rightest thing of all was the dressing-gown. The dressing-gown was terrifically right.'

'Good,' I said unemotionally, noting the point in my mind.

'Well.' Virginia paused, rather teasingly. 'Do you want to know what happened?'

"Yes, *dear.*"

'He crawled in.'

'We guessed he did,' said Janet sarcastically.

'And he crawled up and said "Q5."'

Virginia paused again. We were sitting in a row along the front of the stage, dangling our legs over the edge. I had switched off my torch to save the battery (one must think of overheads in running any business) so it was pitch dark. Virginia was in the middle, her drawly voice coming quietly out of the blackness.

'So he started kissing me.'

'Passionately?'

'Laboured breathing and stuff, yes. Then he started sort of gently jabbing at my front.'

'Outside?'

'Yes. Then he started sort of gently prodding inside. Then he found the dressing-gown cord and undid that. Then he jabbed and prodded and fiddled a bit more.'

'Pyjamas?'

'Outside them. Then he undid one button. Then he didn't know whether to go on. Then he did go on. So he undid all my pyjama coat buttons. So then he was inside.'

'Oh Virginia,' whispered Janet, 'oh Virginia, was it divine?'

'Yes, actually it was,' said Virginia in a matter of fact way.

'Exciting?'

'Riveting.'

'But actually,' I said, 'nice? I mean pleasant? A nice feeling? I mean actually a *pleasant feeling*?'

'Well, of course, it's quite impossible to describe it to *you*, you see.'

'Try,' said Janet.

'Well, tingly. Starting just there and going all over.'

'Goodness.'

'A sort of tingly twitchy, a sort of shivery—'

'Like electricity?'

'Like radioactivity. Everything felt much *bigger*.'

'You mean his hands felt bigger?'

'They felt vast. But I meant, my bosoms.'

'Goodness ...'

'Did you take them *off*, or just have them *undone*?' said Melissa.

'My pyjamas? Well, he sort of hauled the dressing-gown off. And the pyjama top sort of slid off.'

'Cold?'

'*God* no.'

'And the pyjama bottoms?'

'Yes, them, well. He was sort of tickling my tummy—'

'Nice?'

'Absolutely marvellous. And then he found the pyjama bottoms' button.'

'You mean string?'

'No, these button. He tried to undo it, but he couldn't quite get the hang of it. So I did.'

'Quite right,' I said approvingly.

'Well, I quite wanted to.'

'Of course,' sighed Janet.

'So then it was my pants, under that.'

'Pants! We *said* you shouldn't have the pants.'

'Perhaps you were right They surprised him, I think. But he was brave. He—'

'He—'

'His hand sort of wriggled down inside—'

'To—?'

'My tummy still. My *lower* tummy. And then it whizzed round to my behind.'

'Why?'

'I don't know. But he prodded it a bit.'

'Nice?'

'Absolutely heavenly. And then, at that point, I dimly remembered a bit in that book of my papa's.'

'*Prostitution – A Sociological Analysis?*'

'About what they do. They excite The Client. They even undress The Client—'

'Virginia!'

'Well. So I tugged at his shirt buttons. And his hand jumped away from my behind and disappeared. So I thought that meant the next bit was up to me. So I tugged at ID's trouser buttons. Then he began to shiver a bit, which I thought was passion, and then ...'

'Oh Virginia,' breathed Mary-Rose.

'You didn't undo them?' whispered Janet.

'I tried to. Perhaps it was a zip. So I tried to explore down a bit ...'

'Was that nice?'

'I was excited. Yes, I *was* excited. I didn't know quite what I'd find—'

'Yes you did.'

'Yes, of course I did, in theory. But then and there—'

'Yes,' I murmured, 'I see.'

'So then?' demanded Janet.

'That's all.'

'Oh no.'

'He shot away to the edge of the tunnel and wrapped himself up frantically in all his scarves and whizzed off and disappeared.'

'Oh, no.'

'I think I see,' said Mary-Rose very sensibly. 'He hadn't bargained for that. I mean he *literally* hadn't bargained for it. He hadn't paid for it.'

'I believe you're right,' said Virginia slowly. 'He was getting his money's worth just by—'

'Prodding?'

'And rubbing and—tickling and—so on. So I felt silly.'

'Of course. Poor Virginia.'

'Not a wash-out, though,' said Mary-Rose.

'God no.'

'But a lesson,' I said. 'Mary-Rose hit it. Well done, Mary-Rose.'

'Ce n'est rien, cherie.'

'You mean,' said Melissa, 'Q—whatever-he-was—thought he was paying for—'

'Prodding,' said Janet.

'All right,' I said. 'Law of supply and demand.'

'I don't get it,' said Melissa.

'Prodding is a pound.'

'Ah,' said Virginia. 'And, say, just *looking*—'

'Ten bob.'

'And only looking at the top half?'

'Well, and so on. We'll make out a price list.'

'I won't do a thing,' said Melissa, 'for half-a-crown.'

'As for what *we do*,' I said, 'that begins to come expensive.'

'You're a marvel, Boss,' said Mary-Rose handsomely.

'Thank you,' I said. 'Inner Council business discussion tomorrow.'

'Break.'

'History Library.'

'We've got some Cream of Mushroom.'

'Price-list.'

'Scale of charges.'

'Yum.'

Chapter Seven

THE SYNDICATE

LIST OF CHARGES

Vision only:	Above Waist Only	5*s.*
	Below Waist Only	7*s.* 6*d.*
	Entire Operative	10*s.*
Touch:	Above Waist Only	12*s.* 6*d.*

'All agreed so far?'

'Yum.'

'What next? *Touch?*: Below Waist Only?'

'I wonder if there's any point in that?' said Virginia.

'God,' said Mary-Rose, 'that's exactly what there *is* point in'

'But Below Waist Only? Let's go straight to *Touch:* Entire Operative.'

'*Touch:* Entire Operative,' murmured Janet dreamily.

'Yum,' said Melissa again.

So I wrote:

Touch: Entire Operative   15*s.*

'Too cheap,' said Mary-Rose. 'This Entire Operative costs a quid.'

'This is only touching.'

'Well, touching.'

'It's rather a jump,' I said, 'from twelve-and-six to a quid.'

'Then put in *Touch:* Below Waist Only.'

'For the look of the thing. Yes, all right.'

'For the touch of the thing.'

'For the touch of the beautiful *thing*, hee hee.'

'Order,' I said sternly 'Drink up your soup and concentrate.'

'Where do we go, Sarah, where do we go from *Touch:* Entire Operative, one quid?' said Mary-Rose.

'Nothing barred,' said Janet.

'Thirty bob?'

'Two quid.'

'Jolly expensive,' said Melissa doubtfully.

'So I should hope. Speaking for myself, I feel expensive,' said Mary-Rose.

'They do the feeling, dear.'

'*Touch:* Entire Operative.'

'There are lots of sorts of things to fill that gap between one quid and two quid,' said Virginia.

'Such as?'

'Services,' she said obscurely.

'Such as?'

'They're in that book. The real ones do them. And what's more they charge the earth.'

'Ooh, yes. I'm not sure we wouldn't need a bit of instruction.'

'But we ought to offer something at thirty bob.'

'Something between *Touch:* Entire Operative and *Nothing Barred.*'

'Nothing Barred except the—'

'The—?'

'Ultimate,' said Janet.

'I support that,' I said. 'Thank you, Janet.'

'Ce n'est rien, cherie.'

'How do you put it, quite?' said Melissa.

'Nothing barred except, er—'

'Er—'

Melissa giggled. 'The word actually, is penetration.'

'Yes,' said Virginia doubtfully. 'It's a bit clinical.'

'Intimacy, then.'

'Sounds like a story in the *News of the World.*'

'Relations.'

'Sounds like aunts and whatnot.'

'Anyway, it's too vague,' insisted Melissa. 'We've got to say exactly what is barred. Or it's not businesslike.'

'Quite right,' I said.

'Well, but,' said Virginia, 'penetration ...'

'Consummation?'

'Sounds so married.'

'Completion?'

'Like buying a house.'

'Insertion?'

'Shut up, Melissa.'

'Invasion? Intrusion? Inclusion?'

'Shut *up*, Melissa. The bell will go in a sec.'

'Nothing Barred short of ...'

'Damn and blast. There is the bell.'

'La leçon de froggish.'

'How French I feel.'

'Entire Operative feel French?'

'Entire Operative feel très, très française. Some parts of Operative even more than others.'

'What about a French word?' said Janet. 'Nothing Barred short of ... quelquechose.'

'Quelquechose délicieuse.'

'What is the word? Virginia, what's the word in French?'

'There's the second bell,' I said. 'Come on.'

'We'll all think during French.'

'It should be a suitable context.'

'And pool our ideas at the end.'

'Nothing Barred short of ...'

'Come on,' I said, 'come on.'

* * *

'Nothing Barred short of …' said Virginia pensively.

It was two hours later, after odious Games, and we still hadn't solved the problem.

'Thirty bob,' said Janet dreamily.

'Short of …'

'Penetration,' insisted Melissa.

'We can't put that, Melissa.'

'Listen, we must be explicit, right? Because of being businesslike?'

'Right.' I agreed.

'And this is a secret confidential highly confidential document.'

'Yes.'

'Then being a bit clinical doesn't matter.'

'But it sounds so unappetizing,' said Virginia. 'Penetration …'

'La pénétration,' said Mary-Rose vaguely.

'Yes!' said Melissa immediately. It was odd seeing her agree with Mary-Rose like that. The Syndicate, I saw, was a sort of catalyst.

'Yes,' I agreed. 'I think that solves our problem.'

'It makes it more yummy-sounding,' admitted Virginia.

'But just as explicit,' said Mary-Rose.

'Isn't French extraordinary? A couple of accents, and the whole thing's quite different.'

'Yummier.'

'More like thirty-bob's worth.'

'But La Pénetration *as such*,' I said, 'is two quid's worth.'

'Ooh yes. Gumdrops. Do you suppose …?'

'Who knows?'

'Think of Ellis,' said Mary-Rose nervously.

'Perhaps he'll never have two quid,' I said comfortingly.

'Anyway, we can finish the price list.'

'Yes, let's finish the price list.'

I pulled it out and spread it out on the table.

THE SYNDICATE

LIST OF CHARGES

CATEGORY ONE

Vision Only:	Above Waist Only	5*s.*
	Below Waist Only	7*s.* 6*d.*
	Entire Operative	10*s.*

Time limit: 15 minutes

Electric lighting will be provided, and can be
adjusted according to Client's requirements.

CATEGORY TWO

Touch:	Above Waist Only	*12s. 6d.*
	Below Waist Only	15s.
	Entire Operative	£1

Time limit: 30 minutes

CATEGORY THREE

	Nothing Barred Short Of La Pénétration	£1 10s.
	Nothing Barred	£2
	No time limit	

'*The Syndicate Will Meet Your Needs.*'
'*Actions Speak Louder Than Words.*'

'Oh, it's beautiful,' said Janet.

'So what will you do, Sarah?' said Mary-Rose. 'Another conference
with Ellis?'

'God, I suppose so. It's an awful sweat getting there.'

'Write another of your divine business letters.'

'OK, chums.' So I wrote.

Dear Mr Ellis,

The reaction of your Representative Q5 to Mlle Chantal's services
were somewhat disappointing. It appears to The Syndicate that

Mlle Chantal had a different and more mature understanding of the purposes of their meeting in the gym.

'Not half,' said Virginia, looking over my shoulder.

'What a head our Chairman has,' said Melissa.

'We're jolly lucky to have such a super Chairman,' said Mary-Rose girlishly. 'Do you think we should give her three cheers, chums?'

'I think we should.'

They did, raggedly and a bit sarcastically.

'Thank you,' I said, I suppose a bit crossly. 'Now perhaps we can return to business?'

'Of course, carry on.'

'You have quite finished your joke, Mary-Rose?'

'Quite, ta.'

'You're perfectly sure you don't want to amuse us a little more?'

'No no,' she said graciously, 'please proceed with your blissful business letter to the excellent Ellis.'

In order to obviate any repetition of yesterday's evident misunderstanding—

'Obviate!' exclaimed Melissa. 'Boss you're a marvel!'

'Thank you.'

'I would never have thought of obviate. Would you have thought of obviate. Virginia?'

'Never. I take off my hat to the Chairman.'

'So do I,' said Janet, 'and I'm ready and willing, if you really want to know, to take off everything else for the next great burly Client who comes thundering up to the gym.'

'Good,' I said. 'Now, if you will all allow me, I will continue.'

'Yes, what are you waiting for?'

In order to obviate any repetition of yesterday's evident misunderstanding, we beg to enclose our Up-To-Date List Of Charges.

'Very reasonable they are, too,' said Melissa.

'Unbeatable value,' agreed Virginia.

'Shouldn't we have another slogan, Sarah? About unbeatable value?'

'Best Girls, Best Prices,' suggested Mary-Rose.

'They want the worst girls.'

"They got 'em.'

'Highest Quality, Lowest Prices,' said Janet.

'You Can Beat Our Girls, But Not Our Prices.'

'Not me, they can't. Not for thirty bob.'

'Save Today The Syndicate Way,' said Mary-Rose.

'Oh *yes*' said Virginia. 'Masterly, dear.'

'But if they really want to save,' said Janet, 'they needn't come at all.'

'Yes they need. Their growing masculine bodies—'

'Lust and loins and things—'

'Anyway,' said Mary-Rose, 'this is *advertising*.'

'Is it the wish—' I said, feeling I had somehow lost the initiative in what was really, as Chairman, my province – 'is it the wish of the Inner Council that we use the additional slogan—'

'Save Today The Syndicate Way,' intoned Mary-Rose and Virginia in unison.

'I must say it sounds marvellous,' said Melissa. 'Just like those things on television.'

'So go on, Sarah.'

So I went on:

We are convinced that you will agree that our Charges offer Unbeatable Value.

Assuring you of our Best Attention at all times,

We beg to remain,

(For The Syndicate)

S. CALLENDER

'You know what looks wrong,' said Janet thoughtfully, as we read it through together.

'I am sorry anything looks wrong,' I said.

'It's bellissimo, Sarah, every single word, except that one single word "gym".'

'Explicit. Straightforward. Honest.'

'But not romantic'

'Not sexy.'

'There's no throb,' said Virginia, 'or pulsating passion, or anything, in a word like "gym".'

'The best institutions have nice names.'

'Establishments.'

'I mean establishments. The best establishments.'

'I won't have it called "Miss Callender's",' I said firmly. 'No no. More like *The Teahouse of the August Moon.*'

'Ah, I see.'

'The Lotus Blossom.'

'The Passion Fruit.'

'The Budding Passion Flower.'

'It doesn't seem quite complete,' said Mary-Rose. 'The Passion Flower Establishment ...'

'The House of the Budding Passion Flower?'

'The Passion-Flower Hotel?'

'I like that,' said Melissa thoughtfully. 'Passion Flower Hotel. It sounds like a divine sexy novel in a mauve cover you get at Waterloo.'

'The only tiny objection,' I pointed out, 'is that it isn't *exactly* a hotel.'

'*An* hotel is the upper class thing to say.'

'*An* hotel.'

'Anyway,' said Mary-Rose, 'don't be so literal-minded You're becoming too much of a business-woman.'

'Poor Sarah, you'll be a bachelor girl next.'

'Hole and corner cuddles with the boss.'

'Except she is the Boss.'

'Hole and corner cuddles with herself—'

'Worse and worse.'

'Passion Flower Hotel,' said Virginia dreamily. 'It has *poetic* truth, Sarah.'

'Much the best sort,' said Janet. I yielded. One is not obstinate. So I rewrote that sentence.

It appears to The Syndicate that Mlle Chantal had a different and more mature understanding of the purposes of their meeting at The Passion Flower Hotel.

'Yes,' said Janet. 'That looks very nice.'

* * *

So we posted the letter and presently, of course, it was bedtime.

Janet was sitting on the edge of a bath looking at a copy of the List of Charges. Mary-Rose was brushing her teeth Melissa was trying to get her finger-nails clean. Virginia was in the bath, toying languorously with an ersatz sponge. I was trying my hair all over on one side; but it caught in one side of my glasses, so I took them off, and I couldn't see what it looked like from a distance.

'This List of Charges—' began Janet.

'I *love* it,' said Melissa.

'We all love it.'

'I am wondering something,' said Janet.

'What?' I said suspiciously.

'But I don't want to seem *grasping*.'

'So?'

'So all this lovely money, what exactly do we do with it?'

'Two pounds, so far.'

'I am keeping it safe, in trust for The Syndicate,' I said.

'Two pounds,' said Virginia, lazily, from her bath, 'minus the bit for Jungle Venom.'

'And we're going to need more torch-batteries.'

'Well, Sarah?'

'Well what?'

'How do we split it?'

It is difficult to avoid a wrangle on a subject like that, especially with financially immature people like Janet and Melissa. But in the end we agreed that the particular Operative would take half the particular fee she earned, with the rest divided up among the rest of The Syndicate.

'As *originator*—' I began cautiously.

'You earn our gratitude, ducky.'

'Handling the business side is very taxing—'

'The business side, ooh,' said Melissa frivolously. 'Both my sides are business sides.'

'Well, *I* think—' I said.

They all looked at me, and I could see they weren't going to vote in my favour. It never does to risk a responsible position of leadership and trust on a hopeless issue, so I said, 'All right. But of course stamps are a business overhead.'

'You can charge stamps.'

'And stationery.'

'You get that free.'

'And my time?'

'Not your time.'

'Very well,' I said.

Then we were chivvied into bed by a pathetic great prefect called Camilla Beard, to whom I could never bring myself to be cruel because her legs were so pathetically huge and mauve; and then we slept the dreamless sleeps of our innocent girlhood.

* * *

Two days later I got Ellis's reply.

Dear Sarah,

I think your List of Charges is a sensible idea but a bit steep. What about a rate for parties for the Category One things? Above Waist Only could be say 9 bob for two of us, 12*s*. 6*d.* for three, etc. The same with the others. But not Touch, of course, let alone Category Three.

If you agree to this, we have several people for you.

Also it is easier for more than one person to bicycle that terrific distance.

Yours,
H. ELLIS

We discussed this a good deal between Algebra and a new thing they fed our burgeoning minds with once a week called Sociology and Civics.

'But Sociology was not the interesting stuff Virginia's parents' book had led us to expect, being mostly about local government, adult education, shop stewards, and attitude surveys among the labouring classes of the industrial north.)

'I don't know about these cut rates for parties,' said Mary-Rose. 'I don't a bit like the idea of parties.'

'Not orgies. Parties.'

'I'd feel like something in a low joint.'

'Lelia Lulia, The Smouldering Stripper From Tangier.'

'Well, but it's not very refined.'

'It will be very refined,' I said. 'I think it's a money-spinner.'

'Money, yum,' said Melissa.

'Well,' I said helpfully, 'it's no more trouble, it doesn't take any longer, and it means far more delicious dough.'

'Yes,' said Virginia, 'that's the clincher.'

'Well, all right, but then masks.'

'Masks for parties. Yes. Agreed?'

'Agreed.'

'And parties *where*, Sarah?'

'The Passion Flower Hotel.'

'That would be just like a sexy game of sardines.'

'Oh yes. What about the stage?'

'Yes,' said Mary-Rose, 'and then they can keep a respectful distance.'

'Lights?'

'More torches,' suggested Virginia.

'More overheads,' I pointed out. 'Batteries.'

'Worth it, Boss.'

'And the great thing,' said Janet, 'about Category One, is that it will be a sort of trailer.'

'Trailer, Janet dear?'

'A sort of preview. I mean a sort of arouser.'

'Janet is absolutely right,' I said magnanimously.

'Having *seen* Mademoiselle Yvette—'

'Some parts of Mademoiselle Yvette—'

'Why me?' said Melissa.

'They yearn to go on to a quid's worth.'

'Touch: Entire Operative.'

'And then they lust to go on to two quid's worth—'

'Nothing Barred.'

'Help,' said Mary-Rose faintly.

'But Sarah,' said Melissa, 'does whoever it is *go on* to the stage Above Waist Only, say? Or remove something? Or what?'

'Remove,' said Janet instantly. 'More erotic.'

'Why?'

'It just is.'

'How do you know?'

'I just know.'

'She's right,' said Virginia. 'They do. It said so.'

'In *Prostitution – A Sociological Analysis?*'

'The same, old sport.'

Remove bit by bit?' asked Mary-Rose nervously. 'Bras and buttons and things?'

'No. just one thing, I should think.'

'A shirt, just?'

'That's it.'

'With a certain panache,' said Virginia. 'A certain sort of archness.'

'And grace,' said Melissa.

'And subtle invitation.'

'Crumbs,' said Mary-Rose. 'OK.'

* * *

So I wrote to Ellis again, and he wrote back, and we had a party on our hands for Tuesday night. Two parties: Four for Category One: Above Waist Only, at a special rate of sixteen shillings; and no less than *five* for Category One: Entire Operative, at two pounds two shillings and sixpence for the party.

'So we draw lots again.'

'Just between Janet and Mary-Rose and Sarah,' said Melissa.

'Suits me,' said Janet.

* * *

I was let off gym, later that day, because of what a weirdly-frustrated matron female called 'a sniffle.' This suited me very well, gym being so exceedingly hearty and childish and bloomer-clad and even, if one is not careful, a bit sweaty. So, being let off, I went to the History Library and wrote this poem about the frustrated matron female.

TO A SPINSTER

Tragic spreadeagle scarecrows, cap-à-pie,
Armed in some martial sunrise of July,
Keep, on the bitter granite of the fields,
December vigil of an empty sky;
You, whom the summers, once, conspired to bless
Builded your bastions – and have no less
Bars on an empty treasure-house. Becomes
Gesture of virtue gesture of hopelessness.

I copied it out neatly and *gazed* at it.

(I assume you pronounce 'cap-à-pie' in the English way. If it has to be French, of course, we are a bit stuck.)

Then I thought about the Category One operations of the evening at the Passion Flower Hotel, and it was immediately clear to me that poetesses do not do strip-tease acts. *At the very most*, they arrange for others to do them, out of a feeling of service to their friends and Clients.

And then I also thought for a moment about The Syndicate's vote about the division of the money. For the Operative to take half struck me as fair. But for the rest of The Syndicate to divide the rest of the money equally (after deduction of overheads) seemed to me and still seems to me grossly unfair. After all I was the originator and carrier-out and manager and leader and Chairman and Boss and in charge of the whole Syndicate service. I had conducted all the negotiations, by correspondence as well as by personal interview. I had chaired (with firmness and discretion) all Syndicate business discussions. And they weren't prepared to vote me even a slightly bigger cut.

So, I thought, tacking about among the bookcases, so.

I fetched up opposite the row of *England In The Middle Ages: An Introduction For Junior Forms:* the sinister little green books we used for drawing lots. I examined them. I pulled a few out of the shelf and had a very close look indeed. One had a splosh of ink, so of course we would never use it, and one was torn, so we would never use that either. The rest were identical. I pondered for a while, and then ran upstairs and got some nail-scissors, and came back again, and made a little nick in the top of the spine of one of the books.

That, I thought, will show them.

Ha, I thought, so much for mean-spirited followers who deny their leader her due.

It was true, I realised, that I would make less money absolutely, by never having to be an Operative. But also, what was important was that what I made I would make in a purely managerial capacity. Colin was right, after all I *was* different. I would not cheapen myself. I owed it to him, as well as to myself. I would run the joint and take my percentage, as I'd said last term in the hockey-match bus. Ha, I thought, so much for *them.*

Then I heard the others clattering back, so I put the books on the shelf and pretended to be just finishing my marvellous rather obscure poem.

* * *

After tea we drew lots.

I got two bits of paper, and wrote 'You—Above Waist Only' on one, and 'You—Entire Operative' on the other, and then went to the bookshelf for the books.

'Awful little books,' giggled Mary-Rose nervously.

'Courage, petrified-pants,' said Melissa, 'your task is easy.'

'Yes,' said Mary-Rose, 'well. What are we going to do for masks?'

'It may not be you,' said Melissa comfortingly.

'And it may not be me,' said Janet sadly.

I felt quickly and skilfully along the spines as I took the books out, and got the one with the nick on the bottom of the pile Then I put the bits of paper in the top two. Then I moved them about on the table (the croupier's shuffle), keeping a jolly close eye on my special. Then I chose, seeming to do this at the same time as the others. It was quite easy.

Mary-Rose and Janet held theirs up and shook them. I almost forgot to, since I knew nothing would come out. But I remembered, and did, for the look of the thing.

'You—Above Waist Only' fluttered out of Mary-Rose's. 'You—Entire Operative' fluttered out of Janet's.

'Small mercies,' muttered Mary-Rose, apparently *blushing.*

'I'll take everything off *very slowly*, starting at the top,' said Janet.

'I believe you're looking forward to it,' said Melissa wonderingly.

'Yes,' said Janet surprised, 'I bloody well am.'

'Are you, Mary-Rose?'

'What about my mask, I wonder?' said Mary-Rose

'It ought to be interesting.'

'Glam.'

'Catlike.'

'And names for you both?' said Virginia.

'And both at once, in different places? Or one at a time, in the same place?'

'We have a lot to arrange,' I said. 'Business meeting hereby convened.'

So we fixed the details and made our plans.

Chapter Eight

Once again, now very brave, and with a sense of cleverness, I waited at the main gates. It was raining a bit, and extremely dark and beastly, but not too cold. (This was lucky, because goose-flesh all over Janet and Mary-Rose would have been unarousing, as well as horrid for them.)

Presently a lot of murmurs and rustles and gravelly crunchings told me that the Clients had arrived, and I challenged them.

'Who goes there?'

'Us …'

'Well?'

'I mean, for The Syndicate, *you* know—'

'Password?'

'Oh yes. Er, I love my love with a D—'

'Because she is dangerous. Right.'

There is, it became clear to me, a lot of sameness in business. Or in men. Or, in the case of a specialised business like mine, in the one *because* of in the other.

'Follow me, please,' I said. 'Quietly, please.'

'Is it far?' piped a treble voice nervously.

'Buck up, Squeaks,' said a bass voice. 'You'll soon be a man.'

I led them cautiously to the gym, where Melissa challenged us in a dutiful whisper.

'D1 and Clients,' I said.

'Pass, D1 and Clients.'

We got into the gym, and a tall boy with purple spots counted out the money for the Category One: Above Waist Only party. I appraised the four of them: they looked Above Waist Only types – timorous, and rather poor. But probably Janet was right, and they would be aroused, and go on to higher (or lower) and anyway more expensive and delicious things.

Then a squat fair boy, with little beady eyes behind little beady glasses, paid out the huge sum of two pounds two shillings and sixpence for the Category One: Entire Operative party. I counted it, and it was all correct, and it jingled, and weighed my corduroy trousers heavily and marvellously down.

'If the Above Waist Only party will proceed to the front of the hall,' I said grandly, 'Princess Puma is waiting in the wings.'

'Just the job,' said a curly-headed boy in a rather common way.

'What about us?' said one of the Entire Operative five.

'I must ask you to wait outside the theatre until Princess Puma has finished.'

'Hey, in the rain?'

'I know. But it's only fifteen minutes. And you can't see her unless you pay. Perhaps,' I said hopefully, 'you'd like to pay to see her *too*?'

'That rain's ghastly—'

'How much for all of us?'

'Er—under the special circumstances, we can do you a special rate of a pound.'

'*A pound!*'

'That's only four shillings each.'

'I'll stay for four bob,' said a boy who looked like a pastrycook (I mean *clean*, but doughy).

None of the others could, not having four bob.

'Credit?' they said hopefully.

'Terms strictly cash in advance,' I said with regretful sympathy, but firmly. 'And if it's only one, of course, then it's five bob.'

'You said four.'

'That's the special party rate.'

'But I'm joining that other party.'

'Oh, yes. Oh, all right.'

He handed over four shillings, mostly in halfpennies, and shuffled up to near the stage where the others were. I shoo'd the rest outside, and Melissa stood guard over them.

(Virginia, of course, was guarding the other door, and missing all the fun. They had drawn lots, between them, for which door.)

I personally had promised Mary-Rose and Janet that I would stay outside and not watch their performances, except to lean in without looking, to call the time (Time Limit 15 Minutes). But I decided that the smooth operation of the Passion Flower Hotel And Novelty Theatre demanded that I stay inside and supervise the comfort and decorum of our Clients. So I did.

I looked at my watch (actually Janet's – luminous hands). It was twenty-five past eleven. Then I went to the edge of the stage and called up, 'Princess Puma?'

'Pronto,' growled Mary-Rose, hidden behind a wooden bluff, in a strange strip-teaser's voice.

I crept back to about the middle of the gym, and leant on a big vaulting-horse where it would be nice and dark, and I would be nice and invisible, and waited.

We had arranged things rather well. The gym was copiously equipped with thick, prickly coconut mats (you landed on them, as gracefully as possible, after bounding like a bird over the vaulting-horse) which were rolled up and left about when nobody was bounding like birds over vaulting-horses. We dragged two of them to the front of the stage (I mean, of course, near it, and below) and they made quite a comfortable seat. And there, in a sad little row, the Above Waist Only Clients now sat in the darkness.

The stage itself was a bit bare. We had drawn each of the great, dusty, green curtains (one pulled them by huge ropes) about a third of the way across, leaving about a third of the stage visible in the middle. And we put three torches on the stage, propped on bits of wood to make them point upwards, to be footlights. But of course we left these switched off, till The Time, because of the batteries, and overheads, and the profitability of the operation.

So we waited in the darkness.

Then I heard a hoarse little bleat from the stage. 'D1!'

'Someone's calling,' said one of the Clients, turning back towards me.

'Princess Pumice-stone,' said another, and they all laughed in a coarse, nervous way.

'Lights!' said Mary-Rose's funny new voice.

'Check,' I said, and hurried forward and switched on the three torches. They made a nice sort of multiple pool of light for beauty to be displayed in.

'Right, Princess Puma,' I said.

I faded back into the darkness, and there was another long-ish pause. The Clients coughed and the coconut-matting front-stalls rustled under them. The rain was dripping on to a bit of tin somewhere miles above in the roof.

The whole atmosphere was deeply and depressingly unsexy, but somehow in an odd way that made it sexier.

Then Mary-Rose came on.

She was wearing a long skirt, in a kind of off-beige, made of a kind of flannelly material, which we had purloined from a girl called Sandra Laverton. (We took the view that no one, not even Sandra Laverton, could possibly ever want to wear it for *normal* purposes.) This utterly obscured her lower half, right to the ground. On top she wore a cotton shirt, rather Italian and divine and almost-Pucci, taken from another girl so utterly contemptible that we all pretended not to know what she was called. And she was interestingly masked with a sort of bat-winged Venetian mask, made of black thinnish cardboard cut out with nail-scissors and fastened round the back with a bit of black ribbon, which covered nearly the whole of her face and stuck out at the sides.

She really looked very nice in the provocative light of the three unblinking torches.

She sidled on, and stood with her hands on her hips in the middle of the stage, between the two half-drawn curtains, full in the multiple torch-beams.

One of the Clients cleared his throat in a shrill, excited way, and several of them shifted about so that the sausage-roll front-stalls creaked under their eager curiosity.

Then Mary-Rose undid the bottom button of her shirt, and they all seemed to freeze. Then she undid the next, and the next.

There were five buttons in all and even I (who had after all seen Mary-Rose with nothing on dozens of times, and who wouldn't anyway be *interested*) even I was agog.

Then she undid the next to top, and then the top. Then she seemed to stop, and I wasn't sure if this was deliberate or just bashful, but it was very effective.

And then she slowly took the shin off.

Of course, it was just bosom. One bosom, to me, is much like another, though I have to admit that Mary-Rose's is nicely formed. It looked terribly white, and a bit pathetic, but not wobbly, even when she began to walk very slowly to and fro.

The five black heads of the Clients, silhouetted against the torch-beams, were absolutely motionless.

Mary-Rose stood still again, bang in the middle of the stage, in the cream-coloured dusty beams of the footlights. The rain was still dripping on to the bit of tin far above me.

Then she turned very slowly round a few times, and slowly raised her arms above her head. It was terribly quiet, and I made a mental note: soft evocative music next time.

And some son of compere or announcer. Possibly me, or perhaps Virginia, unless she herself was actually performing.

Very, very slowly the minutes ticked by, and Mary-Rose seemed to have run out of Princess Puma gestures. It is difficult to stand on a stage, I suppose, and do nothing in particular, and just be looked at, even if you haven't got anything on Above Waist Only. So I made another mental note: for next time work out a Routine. We would rehearse, and fit to the soft, evocative music. It would be easier for Princess Puma, and better, and more of an arouser.

Meanwhile Mary-Rose was standing rather helplessly, and I thought it must be fifteen minutes. But it was only *four*. We would give her another two, and then she could sidle off again.

So for two more eternally utterly endless minutes she stood about, and turned round once or twice, and raised her arms up, and stood about, and then I called 'Time!'

She sort of jumped, and then whizzed off into the wings.

I walked briskly forward and said, 'Thank you, gentlemen.'

'Thank you,' one of them said in a choky voice.

'But that—' said the doughy-looking one who had paid the extra four bob – 'that wasn't fifteen minutes.'

'So?' I asked coldly.

'It said on your programme. Time limit fifteen minutes.'

'Outer limit,' I said, thinking quickly.

'I paid for fifteen minutes.'

'You are very fortunate to have seen Princess Puma at all,' I said.

'But I paid *four shillings*—'

'Goodness, you've *seen* her,' I said. 'You won't see any more of her if she hangs about up there for another ninety-nine hours.'

'Yes,' said one of the others impatiently, 'come on, Cradders.'

'Anyway, you've got another go,' said another boy.

'I want my money's worth of this go. Or a refund.'

'Quite impossible,' I said.

'Come *on*, Cradders. We don't want to sit here all night.'

Mary-Rose's shirt was still lying on the stage where she had dropped it. I picked it up and threw it into the wings, and a pale figure in the shadows swooped on it and scooped it up and put it on. Then I switched off the torches.

'Princess Puma is tired,' I said diplomatically.

'Oh, all right,' said the beastly one they called Cradders, which I suppose meant his name was Craddock. 'I'll sit tight then, and you poor suckers go out and huddle in the rain.'

'Oh Christmas, to be rich like Cradders,' said the little treble voice.

I led the Above Waist Only party, minus Cradders, to the door of the gym, and they shuffled out.

'Well?' said excited voices, clustering round from the dripping blackness.

'What was it like?'

'Are you a *man* now, Squeaky?'

'Our turn!'

'Come on, men!'

'Follow me quietly, please,' I said.

I got them arranged in the stalls, and switched on the footlights, and looked at my watch – eleven-thirty-four, only nine minutes after Princess Puma had *started.*

'Miss de la Gallantine!' I called softly.

'Ici,' whispered Janet, waiting right at the edge of the half-drawn curtain, and startling me.

I turned to the audience. 'Announcing with pride—Miss Gaby de la Gallantine!'

I faded back again, as was fitting, to my station by the vaulting-horse, and put my glasses on.

And then, almost at once, Miss Gaby de la Gallantine undulated amazingly on.

And twenty minutes later *she was still there.*

We had, in Miss Gaby de la Gallantine – and who would have thought it in a trillion years – a Natural. A Star Is Born – the star of the Passion Flower Hotel And Novelty Theatre, or anyway the Novelty Theatre.

She had ransacked the entire school for her wardrobe, which, as she wore it, was indeed a bit special. She came on in a big white macintosh with the collar turned up, and she held an umbrella open as though it was raining (as it was of course – though not, naturally, in the Passion Flower Hotel And Novelty Theatre). Then the rest you could see was rather dark nylon stockings, French looking, and black high heels which fitted her, luckily, though actually until that evening they belonged to somebody unimportant. And of course a mask, though not nearly as much of one as Princess Puma – just a domino. Rather sexy.

She walked on very slowly, pushing her hips about under the big white mac, right to the end of the stage in front of the curtain, and right back again to the other end, and stood still. Then with a terrific din, she suddenly shut the umbrella, and everybody jumped. And she put the umbrella down. And that was the beginning. Then, without the umbrella, she walked about some more, tremendously hippily, and utterly and completely unrecognizable, and wholly not Janet but some strange stranger called Miss Gaby de la Gallantine.

After a bit she unbuckled the belt of the macintosh, which took about two minutes. The rustle and click of the buckle and belt sounded fearfully loud, in spite of the continual whisper of rain and the drip-drip-drip on the bit of tin in the roof.

In the next twenty minutes, which seemed about two lifetimes, Miss Gaby de la Gallantine removed all her clothes, except just the mask. And then she padded about for a bit, and even did a sort of semi-dance which was incredible, and far beyond the call of duty. And finally she undulated off, leaving bits of clothing and things dotted about all over the stage, as though hit by a Kansas tornado.

The audience, when I ushered them courteously out, also looked like remnants of a tornado in Kansas: broken men. (Broken boys, of course, really.) It was clear that they had been through a great experience, which they would remember all their lives. Even Cradders was silent and abstracted.

I glowed with pride at the Service The Syndicate was offering these luckless celibates in their artificial and monastic predicament; and I gave them all, as they clustered dumbly round the door of the gym, our leaflet.

THE PASSION FLOWER HOTEL AND NOVELTY THEATRE

To Our Patrons
The Management hopes you have enjoyed your evening. If so, please recommend our service to your friends. And if you have any suggestions or criticisms, please let us know. Our aim is to serve you.

Full price-list on application.

Special party rates. Individual requirements catered for.

'The Syndicate Will Meet Your Needs.'
'Actions Speak Louder Than Words.'
'Save Today The Syndicate Way.'

I congratulated Janet later.

'Did you *watch*?' she said.

'You didn't watch me, did you?' asked Mary-Rose furiously

'No, of course not, after I *promised*.' (One must use a good deal of diplomacy with staff.) 'I just leaned in at the end, for the time thing.'

'Ah.'

'But you didn't time my end,' said Janet.

'Well, I met them coming out.'

'What did they say?'

'Nothing,' said Melissa with grudging admiration. 'They couldn't.'

'Ooh,' said Virginia.

'I suppose Janet's aroused them all,' said Mary-Rose crossly.

'I'm sure you did your own more limited performance brilliantly,' I said kindly.

'Well, it was the first time.'

'Mine too,' said Janet, seeming to remember happily.

'I suppose it's your natural bent.'

'Yes, I suppose it is,' agreed Janet placidly.

Chapter Nine

I wrote to Ellis next day, rather subtly I said that The Passion Flower Hotel And Novelty Theatre had seemed to be acceptable to our Clients, and that we were learning all the time, and the next performance would be better still.

He wrote back saying he had another party for Category One: Entire Operative – and probably some for Category Two, and even Three for later on, when people's allowances came through.

Eleven for Category One: Entire Operative. It was obvious from Ellis's letter that they assumed it would be Miss Gaby de la Gallantine again. But I had to put this to the Inner Council.

'If you'd rather not, Janet—'

'Why not?' she said

'Or if anyone else would rather—'

'Janet's obviously very good at it,' said Melissa.

'Hear hear,' said Mary-Rose.

'Anybody else who wants to can have a go,' said Janet generously.

'Perhaps, someone else should *join* Janet,' said Melissa cautiously.

'Two of us?'

'Well, they do. In London. At those *clubs.*'

'The Passion Flower Hotel And Novelty Theatre is not a strip-joint,' I said stiffly.

'Yes, it is,' Virginia pointed out.

'Well, they'll have to pay extra for two.'

'Now you're talking, Boss.'

So I wrote to Ellis again, and it was eventually arranged that Marishka Ibn Hafiz, The Tunisian Thunderball, would join Miss

Gaby de la Gallantine (straight from her triumphs in Paris) for a twenty-five minute performance three nights later, at a special fee of seven pounds ten shillings, for the *eleven* Clients.

* * *

So three nights later, after a wilderness of prep and hockey and other time-wasters, I took the money, mostly in notes, from Ellis. (Ellis himself had come at last. I was glad we had prepared so thoroughly.)

The eleven of them settled themselves into the stalls, and I switched the footlights on. (We now had five torches, as we wanted a bigger pool of soft seductive light for Marishka Ibn Hafiz as well as Miss Gaby de la Gallantine.)

There was a click from behind us in the darkness, which I realised was either Mary-Rose coming in to peep, or Mary-Rose going out again to guard. I tactfully ignored it; one must sometimes turn a deaf ear. Mary-Rose, I thought, might be a bit disgruntled at the way things had gone last time, and we didn't want her doing anything rash like leaving The Syndicate out of pique.

Then I myself faded back, and we all waited. Then soft, evocative music began.

The soft, evocative music came from a portable record-player, belonging to a very young girl, too young to appreciate it, plugged into a lucky electric-light-bulb socket. The record was a rather vulgar LP called 'Strings for Lovers', vol. 2 (belonging to Melissa).

Then a tall figure stepped on to the stage, dressed in tight black trousers and a black sweater, and masked, and extremely sinister.

It was Virginia, and she said, 'Bonsoir, Messieurs, and welcome to ze Passion Flower Otel an' Novelty Theatre. We have a mos' special performance for you zis evening, vhich is—épatant an' completely unique, an' she call 'erself Ze Passion Flower Poker Game.'

'Strip-poker, I hope,' said Ellis loudly, in a bullying and suspicious way.

'Mais oui, but with such a différence,' said Virginia smoothly from the stage. 'Now you all know ze game of poker-dice, yes? An' you know ze game of strip-poker, yes? Zis is strip-poker-dice, alors! Maintenant, c'est l'heure des party-games, an' I wan' two capitaines of ze two teams, compris? You, m'sieur, an' you, m'sieur—'

Very smoothly and efficiently she got two nervous boys to the edge of one end of the stage. They stood peering up at her, wondering what was going to happen to them. Then she produced the big cardboard cube we had spent so long preparing: a single dice (or die?) painted elegantly with the poker-dice symbols: ace, king, queen, knave, ten, nine. It was about nine inches square – big enough for them all to see when it sat on the stage.

Now Virginia explained, in her ridiculous and brilliant broken English, the game we had brilliantly invented, two afternoons before, in the chaste and incongruous surroundings of the History Library, before drawing lots for Miss Gaby de la Gallantine's partner. (I need hardly say I used my marked cards for the draw.)

'Miss Gaby de la Gallantine vill now come on to ze stage on ze left,' said Virginia, and Miss Gaby de la Gallantine duly came in with her extraordinary non-Janet walk. She was wearing a very great many clothes, including scarves and gloves, several bracelets, necklaces, earrings, and oddments. And, of course, her mask.

'An' now,' said Virginia portentously, 'Marishka Ibn Hafiz will come on ze stage also.'

So Melissa came on, also swathed in clothes and jingling and clinking with bangles.

'You, Messieurs—' said Virginia, pointing to the part of the audience in the stalls in front of Miss Gaby de la Gallantine – 'you 'ave ziz mos' lovely mascot. An' if your capitaine win ze round, zen your mos' lovely mascot, Miss Gaby de la Gallantine, mus' take off one clothe—jus' one. And *you*, Messieurs—' she indicated the rest of the audience – 'for you is Marishka Ibn Hafiz. An' if your capitaine win ze round, zen Marishka Ibn Hafiz, zat zey call ze sweet ripe date of Tunis, she mus' take off one clothe Tout compris, chers amis? You 'ave understood, mes capitaines?'

'Yes,' said one captain, much louder than he could have intended.

'I mus' tell you,' said Virginia, 'zat Miss Gaby de la Gallantine an' Marishka Ibn Hafiz 'ave exactly ze same number of clothes, yes? Compris?'

'Fair enough,' said Ellis from the stalls. He seemed to be in Marishka Ibn Hafiz's team.

'Bon. Alors, jouez, mes gars, jouez!'

Team A got a knave, Team B a nine. So Miss Gaby de la Gallantine unravelled one of her scarves from her neck and flung it disdainfully behind her.

Then Team A got a knave again, but Team B got an ace. So Marishka Ibn Hafiz shed her outermost scarf (a common chiffon thing with stupid flowers on it). It was more or less nip and tuck for several rounds after that, with Miss Gaby de la Gallantine taking off her scarves, her beret, both gloves, and the first bracelet, and Marishka Ibn Hafiz (as befitted her savage oriental nature) preferring to kick off her shoes (they pinched, I knew) before proceeding to her scarves and two necklaces.

Now Team A had an impressive winning streak, softly and excitedly cheered by its members. The Team A captain threw a stream of unbeatable aces and kings, and Miss Gaby de la Gallantine lost the rest of her jewellery, her coat, outer cardigan, inner cardigan, and blouse. Then there was another nip and tuck phase, with Marishka Ibn Hafiz also getting down to her petticoat, and taking off her stockings too, and Miss Gaby de la Gallantine reduced to the most inner sort of underwear. The excitement of Team A was mounting. They began to make curious hissing noises, and one of them began to stamp his feet in an overexcited way, until luckily someone stopped him. Team B seemed keen to win, too, but I couldn't honestly see quite why. They all got exactly the same eyeful, whichever team they were on.

Now the dice began to roll for Team B, to the groans of Team A. Soon Marishka Ibn Hafiz was in just about the same condition as Miss Gaby de la Gallantine. And of course it now got rather exciting.

Two remaining garments each, as Virginia pointed out from the stage, and everything to play for.

And it worked out rather luckily. Team B (Marishka's bra, and a sigh from the audience). Team A (Gaby's bra, and another sigh). Team A again (Gaby's knickers, and a sort of groan) And Team B (Marishka's knickers, and another groan).

So they stood there for a bit, posing artistically. Miss Gaby de la Gallantine, as we already knew, was full of confidence and loved her work; and I guessed that having her there, an old trouper, gave Marishka Ibn Hafiz confidence too. I could more or less tell that Marishka was determined to be just as arousing as Gaby, and so, when they began to pace about a bit, she was.

I looked at my watch, and was astonished to see that there were only two minutes to go. Virginia had artfully stretched the poker-dice game to last for twenty-three minutes, and of course having on so many clothes to start with helped also. They only had to walk about and pose for a very short time, which meant that we would have given the Clients their money's worth, without having subjected our artistes to any undue fatigue or humiliation.

So they padded about among the scarves and suspender-belts, and I decided to call 'Time' in another thirty seconds. I took in a breath to do so. And then suddenly there was a clatter, and Mary-Rose was beside me, panting.

'Quick!' she muttered.

'What?'

'Coming!'

'What?'

'Someone's coming!'

'God.'

I slithered to the front and said, 'Clients, into the Hotel. Virginia, get Gaby and Marishka away. Pick up the clothes. Turn the record off. Disappear.'

Gaby and Marishka stood petrified. Suddenly they were Janet and Melissa again, ludicrously and rather rudely standing about on a dusty wooden stage with nothing on.

Then Virginia rushed to the gramophone and switched it off, and went along the row of torches turning them off, and Janet and Melissa frenziedly harvested all their bits – but did not, at this stage, have time to put any of them on.

Meanwhile Mary-Rose was ushering our enormous audience into the big central tunnel under the stage, and telling them to keep quiet. Then she got in too, and I was about to follow her when the far door – the main door of the gym – suddenly opened with a bang.

Perhaps the wind took it. It was lucky that Virginia had switched the footlights off.

I jumped on to the stage and ran out into the wings. The main lights suddenly went on behind me, but by this time I was nipping out of the side door. I stood in the dark for a minute or two, listening for explosions in the Novelty Theatre, and peering round for Virginia, Janet, and Melissa.

But I couldn't hear anything or see anything. So presently, very carefully and slowly, I got back to bed by a roundabout route.

And one by one, after long intervals, the others arrived too.

First Janet. (Trust Janet.) She was fully but rather haphazardly dressed, and holding a lot more clothes.

'Where have you *been*, Janet? Where are the *others*?'

'Last part, don't know. Well, I thought I'd skulk about and see who it was, but I got cold, and I thought I'd better dress, so I did, and here I am.'

'But weren't you with Melissa and Virginia?'

'I lost them. Melissa will be a bit chilly, I've got most of her clothes.'

'Oh goodness.'

'How was the show?'

'Fabuloso assoluto.'

'Yes, I thought the house liked us. Melissa's quite promising, I think, don't you?'

'Very promising,' I said. 'But of course you were the star.'

'Oh yes,' she said, 'I know. I was dreading losing.'

'What?'

'The race. The game. I was determined to win.'

'Why?'

'I don't know. One's competitive instinct. Why does one play games?'

'Seven pounds ten, in this case,' I said coolly.

'Goodness yes, that too! Isn't it divine?' As an afterthought she said, 'I wonder who it was coming and interrupting us?'

'I've been wondering too,' I said.

'Mary-Rose wasn't much of a guard.'

'No,' I said grimly.

'It's a pity we had to stop before the end, too.'

'You only had fifteen seconds to go.'

'Honestly? Oh, well, then, it didn't make much difference.'

'I hope our Clients agree,' I said.

'I should think so. Fifteen seconds isn't much.'

'But we say we guarantee freedom from interruption.'

'For the Hotel, yes. The Novelty Theatre's a different thing.'

'I hope they agree.'

'Anyway, a spice of danger—'

'A spice is all right,' I said. 'Suppose they've been caught?'

'Who's been caught?' panted Virginia anxiously, coming in at that moment.

'We wonder,' said Janet. 'Not us, anyway.'

'What happened?' Virginia asked me.

'Some officious, interfering busybody,' said Janet, 'like some bloody old mistress or something.'

'Where's Melissa?' I said.

'I don't know,' said Virginia in a worried voice. 'I lost her. I thought she was with you, Janet.'

'Not me, no.'

'God, I hope she's all right. She had some clothes, though, didn't she? To put on?'

'Not many,' said Janet. 'She mostly picked up the necklaces and things. I got most of the clothes.'

'God.'

'Anyway, Sarah,' said Janet, 'you've got the money?'

'Oh yes,' I said comfortingly, 'I've got the money.'

'Let's *look at it*.'

So we looked at it: seven pounds ten shillings plus the sixteen and three left (after Jungle Venom) from the first time (Mlle Yvette), plus a pound for the second time (Mlle Chantal), plus three pounds two shillings and sixpence all together for the Opening Night (now so infinitely surpassed) of the Novelty Theatre addition to the amenities of The Passion Flower Hotel.

We were still looking at it when Mary-Rose came in breathlessly.

'God,' she said, sinking on to her bed, 'what a time I've had.'

'Dear little guard,' said Janet viciously.

'Yes, Mary-Rose,' I said severely, 'please explain to us—'

'Oh. Well. Yes. I'm sorry.'

'You were inside?'

'Sort of.'

'You mean you were?'

'Well yes.'

We all looked grave and accusing, and Mary-Rose looked at her shoes.

'I'm sorry, honestly. It was so riveting—you were so riveting, Janet—'

'That's as may be,' I began.

'I don't think she'll do it again,' said Virginia mildly. 'Will you, Mary-Rose?'

'No!' she promised. 'And, oh God, the time I've had.'

'Oh yes, in the tunnel,' said Virginia. 'Rather cuddly, all of you packed in, I should think.'

'Cuddly!'

'Ellis?' I asked sharply.

'He was right at the other end. I could hear him sort of brewing, like a cross kettle. But the ones near me were very unfriendly.'

'Better than being too friendly.'

'Yes … they said our security was bad.'

'It was, dear.'

'I've said I'm sorry.'

'So what happened?'

'There were terrific bumps and footsteps all over the place. Bang over our heads. I must say, boys are very cowardly.'

'That's why we started The Syndicate,' I reminded her.

'Yes, of course …'

'But who was it,' asked Virginia, 'doing all the bumping?'

'Dalton.'

'Oh Mummy.'

Miss Dalton was a sort of policewoman: a superior semi-housekeeper and supernumerary matron who also taught, with awful ferocity, things like Scripture to one or two junior forms.

'Alone?' I said.

'Yes. She found the gramophone.'

'God.'

'And the dice.'

'God.'

'And some earrings, I think. And a scarf, I think.'

'*Which scarf?*' asked Virginia. One of them was hers, and very distinctive.

'I don't know. Anyway, she stumped away in the end, after hours and hours. And so I got the stinking Clients out of the place and beat it.'

'Will they get back to their bicycles?' wondered Janet.

'That or walk.'

'I expect they'll find them.'

'Where's Melissa?' asked Mary-Rose.

'We don't know.'

'Goodness.'

There was nothing we could do about Melissa, as it was pitch dark and the school grounds were extensive; so we waited and talked, and made some more plans, especially about security.

And at last Melissa arrived.

She looked cold and tired, and sore about the feet; she was wearing several bracelets, several necklaces, a scarf, and a floppy hat.

We all babbled at her.

'Oh Melissa—'

'Where have you been?'

'What happened?'

She said nothing, but scrambled immediately into bed, and then began to take off her massed and jingling jewellery, and throw it pettishly about the room. We all fielded bits of it.

It was like a bad-tempered game of rounders in an eastern palace.

'I'm sorry, Melissa,' said Mary-Rose, rather nicely.

'What for?'

'Not guarding very well.'

'It doesn't matter.'

'It does.' Mary-Rose miserably insisted. 'You looked so cold and mizzy coming in.'

'I'm all right.'

'Anyway,' said Virginia, 'you were wonderful, Melissa.'

'Thank you. Was I, Sarah?'

'Intensely arousing,' I said. 'You both were.'

'That's all right, then,' said Melissa more comfortably.

'But where have you been, crazy?' asked Janet, quite solicitously.

'Well, not being very well dressed—'

'You looked marvellous, just as you were, when you came in.'

'Ooh, did I? Yes, I thought just possibly I did, rather, myself. But I thought our sweet superiors might not think so.'

'No,' I said, understanding. 'They don't know about sex and things.'

'It's pathetic, really, isn't it? Anyway,' said Melissa, 'I really couldn't risk being seen.'

'No.'

'So I hung about covertly.'

'You must have been frozen.'

'I froze, yes. You could put me in a packet and sell me. Quick-frozen stripper.'

'Fresh as the moment she was caught.'

'Not boneless,' said Virginia.

'But bloody nearly skinless,' said Melissa. 'I took to the *maquis*.'

'Do you want some Dettol or something?'

'Could you be bothered? I personally can't move.'

So we all turned Nightingale, and bathed Melissa's feet with Dettol, and Mary-Rose filled her own hot water-bottle, and we tucked her up.

'Seven pounds ten,' said Melissa sleepily.

'Non-returnable.'

'We love our work.'

'And we're *good* at it.'

'Except me,' said Mary-Rose.

'Don't mope, ducky. Let's all go to sleep and be pretty and feminine in the morning.'

'Goodnight. Sweet, erotic dreams.'

'Goodnight.'

Chapter Ten

Melissa was sneezing next day, which was annoying but no surprise. Her feet were all right, and so was her morale. The rest of us were fine and, of course, *much richer*.

Thinking it wise, I wrote to Ellis again.

Dear Harold.

The Syndicate was very pleased and gratified you turned up yourself to Patronise The Passion Flower Hotel And Novelty Theatre. I hope you enjoyed it. We all hope you will come again. Miss Gaby de la Gallantine and Marishka Ibn Hafiz both say they noticed you specially, in the audience.

We will, you may be glad to hear, be tightening up our Security Arrangements immediately.

We hope you got back to your transport all right, and were none the worse.

In fact, all the better!

Assuring you of our best attention at all times.

We are,

(For The Syndicate)

S. CALLENDER

'The Syndicate Will Meet Your Needs.'

'Actions Speak Louder Than Words.'

'Save Today The Syndicate Way.'

When I showed it to the others (pretty pleased with it, myself) Melissa said indignantly, 'I didn't notice him specially.'

'They're just a lot of blobs,' said Janet. 'Pale blobs.'

'That bit,' I explained, 'is diplomacy.'

'Ah well, if it's *diplomacy*—'

Melissa sneezed, and we all backed away from her, not wishing to put the entire Inner Council on the sick list and thus have to suspend operations indefinitely. Then she leant back languorously on her pillows and sipped her Ribena as though it was Imperial Tokay.

'Not all that much left of this term,' she said.

'What a term.'

'A whale of a term.'

'Not easy to forget,' said Mary-Rose.

'Thanks to marvellous, wonderful Sarah,' said Virginia, very nicely.

'Hear hear,' said Janet.

'Thank you all,' I said. 'I couldn't have asked for a more loyal and devoted team.'

'Ooh! Really? Us?'

'How,' said Virginia dreamily, 'shall we celebrate the end of term?'

'Us?' asked Melissa, 'as such? Or do you mean The Syndicate as such?'

'Us The Syndicate. That's us.'

'What about a gala show?' said Janet meditatively.

'Packed house—'

'Throbbing, sobbing music—'

'The Passion Flower Follies.'

'Yes! The Passion Flower Follies!'

'Featuring,' said Virginia, 'the Passion Flowers.'

'That's us.'

'Yes,' I said, 'featuring the Passion Flowers!'

'Let's plan.'

'Yum,' said Melissa, 'let's plan.'

Immediately, round Melissa's bed, we eagerly planned.

The way we planned would involve a lot of outlay, but we could find out if it would be worth it. Ellis would know. Longcombe probably felt at least as end-of-term at the end of term as we did; and if they did we could book solid at ten shillings a head.

'How many,' said Janet, 'at ten shillings a head?'

'Dozens.'

'Hundreds.'

'Do you think we'll have to pay Entertainment Tax?'

'No,' I said judiciously, 'I don't think we will.'

'Costumes,' said Janet. 'We steal, yes?'

'Borrow.'

'Cut up.'

'Cut *down*.'

'Perhaps even *sew*,' said Virginia.

'N'exagérons pas, cherie.'

'Music?'

'Our schoolmates are made of L.P.s.'

'Acts and Numbers?'

'Set Pieces?'

'Routines?'

'Specialities?'

'We will devise them all,' I promised.

'I like the idea,' said Melissa, 'of Specialities.'

'Get well soon, to be a Speciality.'

'All right,' she agreed.

'And we'll have a marvellous programme.'

'A collector's piece.'

'A connoisseur's piece.'

'Can you do a connoisseur's piece on school writing-paper?'

'We can, chums. It's all a question of wording.'

'Yum.'

'And look,' said Virginia, '*look*.' She wrote something down and showed it to us.

The Passion-Phlower Phollies.

'Oh how sweet,' sighed Mary-Rose. 'Oh—how—*sweet*.'

* * *

Half way through the morning we had English, and I was reading aloud to the rest of the class my essay on lyric poetry.

I was just getting to a specially well-written and passionately-felt bit so it was particularly annoying when a suet-pudding of a prefect came in and whispered something to Miss Carrington.

Carrier-pigeon nodded and sent her away again, and then interrupted me.

'Yes, Miss Carrington?' I said brusquely.

'You're to go and see Miss Abbott at once, dear.'

'Why, Miss Carrington?' I asked, my voice suddenly a bit hoarse and my throat dry and my heart going bump-bump-bump.

'No doubt she will tell you, Sarah.'

'No doubt.' I said.

I caught Virginia's eye, and Mary-Rose's. Janet was away-over on the right, and Melissa in bed with her cold; but two pairs of eyes was quite enough to mirror what I felt myself: panic.

They've got our fingerprints on the dice or something.

Expulsion, disgrace, facing my parents.

I felt a bit sick, and cleared my throat loudly, and bumped into a few desks on my way out.

The suet-pudding prefect was waiting for me outside.

'Come on,' she said, 'what have you been up to?'

'Poetry,' I said. 'Hockey. Usual stuff.'

My voice sounded a bit more normal to me, but not quite absolutely right. I thought I had better practise it, so I would be innocent sounding when I got to Miss Abbott, so I went on: 'And what have *you* been doing? Not poetry I expect, but I expect lots of hockey and Latin and things? I expect lots of French and things too? And sewing and Alusic Appreciation—'

'Shut up,' she said, like a weak-minded corporal. 'Quick march.'

'Left right left right,' I babbled wildly, as we walked the long walk along parquet floors, and some marble, and some pinkish concrete, to the Headmistress's study.

(If I make this episode sound *at all* comic, it is wrong. I was very frightened and feeling ill, like having the curse plus going on the Scenic Railway at a funfair.)

Suet-pudding knocked on the big shiny door, and Miss Abbott's hooty voice said, 'Come in.'

We went in.

'Thank you, Barbara,' said our beloved Head to suet-pudding.

Suet-pudding smirked and hung about.

'I will talk to Sarah alone, dear,' said the old bag, so suet-pudding wobbled out and shut the door tidily, in a boring and well-conducted way.

I had been looking down demurely at a stupid leather waste-paper basket, but now I raised my eyes courageously to face Miss Abbott. I tried hard to fill them with innocent frankness. I wondered whether to take my glasses off, but I decided to keep them on: one is a tiny bit more *forewarned* if one can see properly – things can come at you with unfair suddenness out of a blur – and also I thought I might look more serious-minded and scholarly with them on.

(They are quite nice glasses, and expensive of course.)

The first thing I saw gave me a horrible jolt. It was our beautiful dice. It lay near the edge of the big shabby desk, on top of a pile of essays (pathetic, immature compositions, no doubt, though submitted with ludicrous pride by much older girls than I). The king was on top, with rather a sly face. The queen accusingly faced me. Mary-Rose had drawn them, which she is quite good at.

When I saw this horribly accusing dice I could feel myself beginning to blush. It came pounding up my neck and all over my cheeks and started banging in my forehead. It must have been visible thirty miles away, like a beacon announcing disaster.

'This object, Sarah. Have you ever seen it?'

'Yes, Miss Abbott.'

'Tell me about it.'

'It is a kind of dice.'

'Go on.'

'I don't know why we made it, really. We all like doing things with our hands, and one can't sew all the time. It is not to *gamble* with, Miss Abbott.'

'At any rate, you admit it is yours?'

'Ours. Oh yes, Miss Abbott.'

I am naturally extremely truthful, and not at all given to telling lies, even to protect myself.

'Now can you tell me why, Sarah, Miss Dalton should have found it on the stage of the gym last night?'

'No, Miss Abbott.'

(Truth should not become an *obsession*. And I had to sacrifice my principles to protect my followers. This is leadership.)

'I think, I last saw it the day before yesterday. But it may have been yesterday. I'm not sure where. Perhaps we left it in the History Library.'

'And this gramophone, Sarah?'

'I don't know who that belongs to, Miss Abbott.'

'And these earrings?'

'I think Melissa has a pair like that. I don't think she ever wears them They were given to her. We are all too young for earrings, Miss Abbott.'

'And this scarf?'

'Oh yes,' I said with tremendously engaging frankness, 'I'd recognise that anywhere. It's Virginia's. She will be pleased it's turned up—she lost it last week and she was miserable. As a matter of fact she *thinks* ...'

'Yes, dear?'

'I don't think I'd better say, Miss Abbott.'

'I require you to tell me, Sarah.'

'I don't want to seem a sneak,' I said stoutly, in my Angela Brazil voice.

'That does you great credit,' said Miss Abbott in a dry and rather sinister voice. 'Now please stop prevaricating and tell me whatever you started to tell me.'

'Well,' I said, 'it's only what Virginia thinks. She thinks it was pinched.'

'By whom does she think it was stolen?'

'That, Miss Abbott,' I said firmly, 'I simply can not tell you. It was only a suspicion.'

'I see. Hm,' she paused, perhaps baffled, but perhaps (I thought, still in terror) preparing her next grenade. 'High spirits I can understand, Sarah.'

'High spirits, Miss Abbott?'

'Such as, to give you an example of stupid and selfish, but not downright wicked, behaviour' – she lost the thread of her complicated sentence, and said sharply – 'midnight feasts?'

'We are not in the kindergarten, Miss Abbott,' I said, shocked.

'You are not helping me, Sarah.'

'I'm sorry, Miss Abbott. How can I help you?'

'Don't be impertinent. You are in very serious trouble.'

I saw, sickeningly again, that I was.

'Sorry,' I mumbled.

'I have very grave suspicions, Sarah—'

'Yes,' I tried to say, engagingly frank again, but nothing very much came out.

'While I am not able to prove or pin down—'

'Ah,' I said softly.

I felt, like cold water rushing into a slight-too-hot bath, a blessed flood of relief She didn't *know.* She only *guessed.* Let her guess, poor old innocent.

'May I ask you, Miss Abbott …?'

'Yes?'

'What do you suspect us of?'

She looked at me magisterially (I suppose) and said nothing for a bit. Because, of course, she didn't know what to say.

At last she pronounced: 'I strongly advise you to be careful, Sarah. Careful in what you say to me.'

(I will, old tortoise, I thought.)

'… and very, very careful in your behaviour from now on.'

(I will be, you bet, I thought.)

'I'm simply warning you, Sarah. I have got my eye on you.'

'Yes, Miss Abbott,' I said meekly.

'The second thing is this. I have, as I say, no actual proof that you and your friends are breaking any rules—'

'Then—' I began bravely.

'Be silent. But as I said to your mother last term, you five are altogether too much of a clique. It is thoroughly bad for you all. None of you, I must continue to hope, are really vicious or antisocial, but as a clique your influence is deplorable. You have a bad effect on each other.'

'I don't *think*—' I began, alarmed but still brave.

'Be quiet, child. I have decided to split you up, whether you like it or not.'

'Split us up!'

'You are all in the same form, which I can do nothing about. And if you choose to spend your free time together I should find it difficult to stop you entirely. Though I may say I intend to try. But you are also all in the same dormitory, and this at least can be remedied.'

'But, Miss Abbott—'

'Will you please stop interrupting me? I am entrusted by your parents, with your education and welfare, and I should be failing in my duty if I did not do what I thought needful to protect you from yourselves and each other.'

'But Miss Abbott—'

It was a severe blow. We had spent many terms of unremitting intrigue to get ourselves, with no outsiders, into that special and unique little dormitory. And now Virginia was to move upstairs among some seniors. Mary-Rose was to move sideways to some girls of our own age, but contemptible. Melissa was to move downstairs among some juniors. And Janet and I, alone of the Inner Council of The Syndicate, were to stay where we were.

'Who will move in?' I asked helplessly.

'Some extremely nice girls, with whom I require you to become friends.'

'Such as?'

'Don't cross-examine me, Sarah. You are in no position to be defiant.'

'No, Miss Abbott.'

'You have not, owing to some oversight for which I blame myself, had a prefect in that dormitory. This we shall put right.'

'What prefect, Miss Abbott?'

'Cordelia Symington.'

Cordelia! The hockey-captain with the bolster-bosom. Mary-Rose's chum, since they were both in the team together. A sporty, virtuous, hearty, Christian girl, the pride of her mother (no doubt) and the admiration of the school. The worst possible.

'Oh good!' I said girlishly.

'And remember, Sarah—and pass this on, please, to your friends …'

'Yes, Miss Abbott?'

'You are being watched.'

'Yes, Miss Abbott.'

I went out, holding my head high, but thinking furiously.

* * *

I should, by the rules, have gone straight back to Miss Carrington's English class. But I reasoned that they would, after so long an interruption, have lost the thread of my essay on lyric poetry. And I didn't want to disturb them. So I went to our dear History Library and pondered.

As I saw it, we had three possible courses open to us under these new Nazi restrictions.

First, we could take the profit we had got and disband The Syndicate. The Passion Flower Hotel And Novelty Theatre could shut its delicious doors for ever. Our clientele would have to do without us. We ourselves would have to restrict our serious education to the holidays.

This was unthinkable. The Show Must Go On.

Or, second, we could carry on with our personnel as it was, and just proceed with infinite stealth. This would be desperately difficult. Perhaps impossible. Exceedingly dangerous.

Or, third, we could get the co-operation – active or passive – of the people in our various dormitories. Not necessarily all, and not necessarily in The Syndicate, but just keeping quiet and letting us get on with it.

This would not be easy, I realised, but *possibly* possible. It would need a mixture of bribery, blackmail, threats, cajolery, and other advanced techniques. But without them the Syndicate Service was at an end.

I was perplexed and dismayed.

When my colleagues emerged from English, we all went upstairs (it was Break) to the sick-room to console Melissa. I told them the news, and they were horrified.

'Alone among a lot of elderly spinsters,' moaned Virginia.

'Alone among a lot of nameless wets,' moaned Mary-Rose.

'Alone among a lot of drivelling brats,' moaned Melissa.

'Just us, alone among Cordelia Symington, and none of you,' moaned Janet.

'It's going to make things difficult,' I said gravely.

'Totally utterly imposs.'

'We're out of business.'

'Bolt the doors of The Passion Flower Hotel.'

'Ring down the curtain of the Novelty Theatre.'

'God, what a shame.'

'It's unfair!'

'It's just not fair!'

'Courage,' I said.

'Ideas, Boss?'

'Perhaps,' I said. 'Listen. Virginia, Mary-Rose, Melissa – find out the names, all the names of all the girls in all the dorms you're going to.'

'They will be quite unfamiliar to me,' said Melissa austerely.

'Nevertheless.'

'And Janet, can you find out exactly who's coming in with us?'

'Yup.'

'We'll convene an Extraordinary General Meeting of the Inner Council after prep, and discuss.'

'Discuss what?'

'Plans. Ways and means. But we must have those lists. Above all the prefects and things.'

'Are we going to rub them out?'

'No. Enlist them in.'

'Sarah! You're joking! All of them?'

'Enough. Enough to ensure silence.'

'But,' said Mary-Rose, '*Cordelia*?'

'She may be a special job for you, Mary-Rose.'

'But ... doing a dance, Sarah? Or Category Two? With Ellis?'

'Perhaps not Ellis,' I said. 'But she may well be some rough rugger-player's ideal.'

'We are talking about the same girl? Cordelia? The Cordelia I know? The one with the bosom?'

'The same.'

'Though mark you,' said Virginia, '*girl* is stretching it a bit.'

'We either buy silence and co-operation,' I repeated patiently, 'or The Syndicate is out of business.'

'Co-operation,' said Janet. 'You mean participation? Or not?'

'Perhaps.'

'Not Cordelia,' repeated Mary-Rose doggedly, 'not Cordelia.'

'But Sarah,' said Melissa, 'why does she suspect us? How did she guess?'

'She didn't, really,' I explained. 'Not specifically. She just knows we're up to something.'

'But we're not,' said Janet, 'we're not up to anything that does anybody any harm—'

'Quite the reverse.'

'Or breaking school property or anything—'

'Or even breaking bounds.'

'They got us on the dice, of course. That was the tip-off.'

'My lovely knave,' said Mary-Rose.

'I liked your king best,' said Virginia.

'He was a sexy old beast, wasn't he?'

'And then,' I said, 'also there was the gramophone and the scarf.'

'They couldn't have guessed much from the gramophone.'

'Just playing records, they might have thought.'

'Just high spirits. Nothing wicked.'

'What a bore it would be just having high spirits, nothing wicked,' said Melissa.

'By the way, Virginia,' I said, 'you lost that scarf last week, and you thought it was pinched, but nothing will induce you to say who you thought pinched it.'

'Plucky little topper that I am.'

'Hear hear. A real chum.'

'Quite likely the most popular girl in the fifth.'

Virginia agreed warmly. 'I wish there were more like me.'

'The world would be a better place.'

'But they don't make many like Virginia any more.'

'Very few. Tragically few.'

'I don't know why we're all being so damn jolly,' said Melissa. 'This is a desperate moment.'

'The Syndicate will not admit failure,' I said sternly. 'We are in business! Courage! Resolution!'

'We shall thrive on difficulties.'

'No,' said Melissa, 'we shan't. Everything made easy is what we should thrive on.'

'Category Two,' said Janet dreamily, her mind obviously going along tracks of its own.

'Category Three …' squeaked Mary-Rose.

'List of Charges …'

'For Cordelia,' said Mary-Rose, 'we should *have* to charge extra, whatever the Category.'

'As Skipper of the Hockers Side?'

'She could slowly remove her shin-pads, and then her blazer—'

'It would be different. A new approach.'

'But I don't know how we explain it to her.'

'Your job, Mary-Rose. You are her chum.'

'It's true. I am her chum.'

'Then.'

'Oh Mummy, imposs.'

'Not persuadable? By her chum? Her right-winger?'

'Cordelia? Ask yourself a little.'

'Then blackmail.'

'What blackmail?' said Virginia. 'If ever I saw a girl who led a totally blameless life—'

'Don't you believe it,' I said. 'We'll find a way! Courage!'

'Oh Boss, you are a comfort.'

'C'est mon métier.'

'And mon métier,' said Melissa, 'is—'

'Is—?'

'The Passion Flower Hotel And Novelty Theatre.'

'And so say all of *us.*'

Chapter Eleven

We spread all the lists of all the girls in all our dormitories gloomily on Melissa's bed in the sick-room. Then we stared at them.

'The little chickabiddies I am to go among,' said Melissa, 'when I am recovered of my grievous distemper, are apparently in the region of twelve or thirteen years of age. Too young for love.'

'Nymphets?' suggested Virginia.

'Come, come! The gentlemen would not put up with it.'

'And your dormitory prefect?' I asked.

'Margaret Renton.'

'Gum.'

Margaret Renton was spotty and scholarly, and bound for Girton, and would not have known what to do with a lipstick if it had been handed her, with instructions in Ciceronian Latin, on a platinum platter.

'Trouble,' I said. 'Virginia?'

'I suppose my poor old doddery companions are all about seventeen.'

'They wear woolly bedsocks, one supposes.'

'They crochet.'

'Too old for love.'

'We'll see, we'll see.'

'My lot,' said Mary-Rose, 'are all, without a single solitary exception, far and away infinitely too *ugly* for love.'

'Prefect?'

'Felicity McBean.'

'Oh dear.'

'Perhaps we could put them all in as bargain-price rejects?'

'For the poorer boys?'

'Not in our beautiful Passion Flower Hotel,' said Virginia, shocked. 'Not bargain-price rejects.'

'Then we'll open another establishment. What they call a cat-house.'

'That idea,' I said thoughtfully, 'has certain possibilities. Now, as for us, Janet—?'

'Cordelia Symington,' said Janet gloomily.

'Oh God. Isn't it unfair?'

It was difficult. We pondered and planned for a long time.

* * *

At first we got nowhere. Virginia talked subtly with the elderly sub-debs in her new home. But the problem was that

'when I am recovered of my grievous distemper, are apparently -in the region of twelve or thirteen years of age. Too young for love.'

'Nymphets?' suggested Virginia.

'Come, come! The gentlemen would not put up with it.'

'And your dormitory prefect?' I asked.

'Margaret Renton.'

'Gum.'

Margaret Renton was spotty and scholarly, and bound for Girton, and would not have known what to do with a lipstick if it had been handed her, with instructions in Ciceronian Latin, on a platinum platter.

'Trouble,' I said. 'Virginia?'

'I suppose my poor old doddery companions are all about seventeen.'

'They wear woolly bedsocks, one supposes.'

'They crochet.'

'Too old for love.'

'We'll see, we'll see.'

'My lot,' said Mary-Rose, 'are all, without a single solitary exception, far and away infinitely too *ugly* for love.'

'Prefect?'

'Felicity McBean.'

'Oh dear.'

'Perhaps we could put them all in as bargain-price rejects?'

'For the poorer boys?'

'Not in our beautiful Passion Flower Hotel,' said Virginia, shocked. 'Not bargain-price rejects.'

'Then we'll open another establishment. What they call a cathouse.'

'That idea,' I said thoughtfully, 'has certain possibilities. Now, as for us, Janet — ?'

'Cordelia Symington,' said Janet gloomily.

'Oh God. Isn't it unfair?'

It was difficult. We pondered and planned for a long time.

At first we got nowhere. Virginia talked subtly with the elderly sub-debs in her new home. But the problem was that they thought (old innocents!) she was too young to be taken seriously on such matters. Mary-Rose reported that the ill-favoured but right-aged creatures she was now among simply never understood her hints; and this was a problem too, because if one said any of it explicitly, then everyone would know, and would tell, and it would be disaster. If one hinted they would be foxed and baffled and utterly in the dark.

(It all, as Mary-Rose sensibly pointed out, showed how necessary and how overdue the Syndicate service was, not only for our Clients but for us too.)

Melissa, of course, had only her prefect to work on; her new little friends were, we thought, too young either to participate or to give us much trouble. But the prefect being the bluestocking Margaret Renton, we had smallish hopes. But when she (Melissa) was better she would have to try her best.

And Janet and I, as well as Mary-Rose, started skilfully working on Cordelia Symington. This appeared to us foredoomed. Even my courageous hopes were pretty dashed. Her great square solid bosom blocked all advances. She was not a girl you could hint to about anything, let alone love. And it was impossible to imagine her in a tender and seductive role in The Passion Flower Hotel.

It was all rather sad and dismaying.

* * *

Then we got another letter from Ellis.

Dear Sarah,

Thank you for yours to hand.

I must say last night was 1st Class, but this business of somebody coming in is a bit off. If you had a guard on, what was she doing? Anyway thank God it was only a Category One. I hate to think of those two stark naked in the cold out there in the dark.

We note you are tightening up your security arrangements. High time if I may say so, a few more near things like last night and we shall all be expelled.

I have pleasure in informing you that I have 2 Clients Category Two: Entire Operative. The sooner the better.

This request is on the strict understanding that security will be 100 per cent.

Yours,

H. ELLIS

PS. I need hardly point out that if in the near future a Category Three is called for we must rely absolutely on security which has got to be 100 per cent, since, to put it baldly, we will be undressed. Anyone coming in then would be The End.

Yours,

H. ELLIS

'We will now draw lots,' I said.

I tore Ellis's letter in half, and put one half in each of two copies of *England In The Middle Ages: An Introduction For Junior Forms.* Then I shuffled five copies about, watching my precious marked one.

Then we picked. It was just as solemn as always. Out they flew: it was Mary-Rose and Virginia.

'Funny,' said Mary-Rose, 'how you never win, Sarah.'

'Yes,' I said.

'I mean it is rather funny.'

'Yes, it is,' I said, 'very funny.'

'Are you sad?' asked Virginia.

'Of course she is,' said Janet.

'Of course I am,' I said.

'Would you like to swap?' said Virginia. 'I've done this sort of thing once, you know—'

'And very well too,' I said quickly.

'... and I don't want to be selfish.'

'You got The Passion Flower Hotel properly started.'

'Thank you, Boss, for those few kind words.'

'But Sarah,' said Mary-Rose rather persistently, 'it is about your turn.'

'No no,' I said graciously, 'it's the luck of the draw. I'll win soon, I expect.'

'I hope so,' said Janet kindly.

'So do I,' said Mary-Rose.

* * *

The arrangements were tricky. First we had to fix up another chambre d'amour in The Passion Flower Hotel, which meant more luxurious dusty drapes from round and about the stage, and more torches sexily dimmed with coloured Cellophane over the glass.

And then there was the problem of how to escape and foregather.

Melissa, naturally, was out of it even as a guard or box-office girl. We all agreed that she must stay in bed and get better and back on duty. So we could beg the question, for the moment, of coping with Margaret Renton.

Mary-Rose had to work on her prefect Felicity McBean, and Felicity McBean was a pill. She was one of those long-nosed girls with mauve legs and a sense of duty. So what we planned was rather sly. Before Melissa left the sick-room, she managed to pinch two sleeping-pills (long shiny red things) from the lock-up chest in the Matron's room, next door to the sick-room she was in. Virginia said they were perfect because, apart from being sleeping-pills, they were also phallic symbols, and so might subtly influence Felicity McBean into more civilised attitudes. Mary-Rose had to undertake to get them, somehow, inside Felicity McBean.

'How?' asked Janet.

'God knows.'

'Gild the lily,' said Virginia. 'I mean sugar the pill.'

'I don't suppose', objected Mary-Rose, 'Miss Mc'bean ever eats sugar.'

'I bet she eats chocolates.'

'Now that,' I said generously, 'is a good idea. A *very* good idea.'

'We'll blue a bit of the profits on a box of Black Magic—'

'Insert our phallic bombshells—'

'And Mary-Rose, sucking up girlishly to her new dorm pre—'

'You are a great help, Virginia,' I said, 'a most valuable member of The Syndicate.'

'Ooh *am* I?' she cried 'Ooh good!'

So we went to what they called the Tuck Shop (in pathetic imitation of boys' schools) but they had no Black Magic: only Cadbury's Milk Tray.

'Black Magic would be better,' said Virginia dubiously. 'Sexier.'

'Make the day, make the day, with Cadbury's Milk Tray,' sang Mary-Rose.

'Then you do watch television,' I said sharply. 'You pretended you never did.'

'I saw that in the cinema. Make the day—'

'Spare us the adverts, dear. Come along and doctor Felicity's goodies.'

This turned out to be much more difficult than we expected. First we tried putting a whole pill, in its red capsule, inside a squishy-centred one, but then we realised she would bite on it as soon as she began to chew, and spit it out, and not be sent asleep. So then we opened up a pill, and tried making little holes in the chocolates and pouring the magical powder in. But the difficulty was making room inside the chocolate for the powder. They were all full of delicious goos and nuts and whatnot; we had to hollow them out. But if you have ever tried hollowing out a chocolate you will know what a mess you make. In the end we tried cutting them in half and sticking them together again The result was a bit amateurish, but all right (we thought) except under a strong light. Mary-Rose promised to offer the chocs to Miss McBean under a weak light.

Finally, after all our experiments, we had very few chocolates left, so we put just the two doctored ones in the top layer, and the poor remainder below, and our trap was baited.

That looked after Felicity McBean.

Next we considered Virginia's escape. Very luckily all her older dormitory-mates had been rather upstage with her, and had made her have a rotten bed just by the door. (I mean its position, for law-abiding slobs like themselves, was rotten, as it was by the door. The bed itself was like the other beds: rotten, to be sure, but no worse than the rest.)

'So I think I'll just slink,' said Virginia.

'You must be very careful opening the door,' said Melissa.

'And very careful shutting the door,' I said.

'I will. The only one I'm alarmed about is Meg Lavington.'

'To be alarmed about Meg Lavington,' I said, 'is to be alarmed about life.'

'Very clever, ducky I mean she has the next bed to me.'

'What bliss for you both,' said Mary-Rose.

'Near, Virginia?' I said, returning to business.

'Pretty near. I'll just have to be mouselike, and hope.'

'We'll all be mouselike. And we'll all hope.'

Finally there was the awful problem of Janet and me. All we could do was have another go at Cordelia Symington.

'More sleeping-pills for Cordelia?' suggested Virginia.

'We've used them up.'

'Melissa could get some more.'

'No,' said Melissa. 'Melissa couldn't.'

'She has been ill,' I explained.

'I am still ill.'

'Besides,' said Mary-Rose, 'you would need a barrel of the stuff to sink Cordelia.'

'Could we learn hypnotism and hypnotise her?'

'There isn't time. Anyway it would be like trying to hypnotise Burlington House. She is too solid to hypnotise.'

'Violence?' suggested Janet.

'She is too strong,' I pointed out.

'Then you must blandish,' said Virginia. 'Blandish or creep.'

So, a bit later, in the dormitory, two hours before our Clients were due, we desperately blandished.

'High spirits are not vicious, Cordelia,' I began smoothly, 'are they?'

'What are you talking about?' she said in her rough, rather paternal way.

'I mean we are not vicious. But we are a bit high-spirited.'

'Not while I'm around.'

'We are young, Cordelia. For the first and last time we are young—'

'Look, I expect you've been having pillow fights and I don't know *what* goings on in here. But that's all got to stop.'

'It will!' I promised with devout sincerity. 'We promise never to have another pillow fight, don't we, Janet?'

'Yes, we swear,' said Janet, sadly but contritely.

'But what harm is there—' I went on cajolingly – 'I mean, in a walk at night? The moon—'

'It's raining.'

'The rain, then. Do you realise how much poetry there is—'

'If you're thinking of going for a walk tonight,' said Cordelia sternly, 'I strongly advise you to chuck the idea. I'll be on you like a ton of bricks.'

'Of bricks, Cordelia?'

She laughed in a quite good-humoured way, gruffly, like an uncle who smells of pipe-smoke, and said, 'A ton of me, then. And you better learn not to be so blooming cheeky.'

'We will, Cordelia.'

'Now get undressed and be quick about it.'

Janet and I looked at each other, and Janet shrugged imperceptibly. It was creep, then. Mouselike stuff. Very alarming.

* * *

Two hours later we crept. Our clothes for the evening were already (by our usual marvellous forethought) in the bicycle-shed, so all we needed to take was macintoshes. It was easy. We opened and shut the door very slowly and silently, and the deep-breathing noises from round and about went on uninterruptedly.

When we got to the bicycle-shed (sprinting the last bit, through the drizzle), Virginia was already there.

'Good creeping?' she asked.

'Faultless creeping. And you, Chantal?'

'Absolument parfait. Where's Mary-Rose?'

After rather a long time Mary-Rose appeared.

'I'm sorry,' she said immediately, 'I'm out of it tonight.'

'But Mary-Rose—'

'Miss McB. is wide awake and suspicious.'

'*No. Imposs.*'

'Didn't she eat the chocs?' asked Virginia, horrified.

'Oh God,' said Mary-Rose wearily, 'no, she didn't. You know how *nice* she is? How good an example she sets to us all?'

'Go on,' I said, with a sense of foreboding.

'She was too generous, too unselfish, to eat my chocolates. I pressed them on her—'

'How unnatural if she refused. How rude.'

'She said no, no—they're yours, Mary-Rose. I said no, no—I hated chocs, I was forbidden chocs—'

'Clever Princess Puma.'

'So in the end they went to two greedy little girls whose names need not concern us.'

'Oh God,' said Virginia, 'so two nameless, faceless creatures are deeply and soundly snoring—'

'And Miss McB. is wide awake,' I said glumly.

'Oh God. It's not fair!'

'So when I crept out' – went on Mary-Rose – 'she sat up and asked where I thought I was off to.'

'You should have said the loo.'

'I *did* say the loo, clever. But the loo doesn't take long.'

'It can do,' said Janet. 'I remember once—'

'Spare us, dear. Anyway, it can't possibly take as long as The Passion Flower Hotel.'

'No.' I agreed. 'I suppose she'll stay awake?'

'Ask yourself.'

'She's utterly unnatural,' said Virginia, 'this Miss McB. First refusing a kind and thoughtful present, then staying awake all night—'

'She's a problem we shall have to solve.'

'And meanwhile she's waiting for me. I must get back,' said Mary-Rose.

I rapidly saw we should have to find a substitute for Princess Puma. Janet or me. And they would expect it to be me. So suddenly and violently I pretended to sneeze.

'I seem to be getting a cold,' I gasped.

'Oh *Sarah*—'

'Melissa's, I expect … I was just going to volunteer to take Mary-Rose's place—'

'You'd better not,' said Janet instantly.

'I'm honestly afraid,' I said with pitiful misery, 'I'd really better not.'

'Janet will cope,' said Mary-Rose. 'Good luck, chums. Sorry to let you down.'

'All that money on those chocs,' moaned Virginia. 'Goodnight, Mary-Rose.'

Mary-Rose scampered off through the streaming darkness, and Janet said, 'I'm not very glam for the Passion Flower Hotel.'

'You will be,' said Virginia, 'as soon as you're Entire Operative.'

'Ooh, yes I'll just wear this mac.'

'All you need. *More* than you need.'

'Masks?' I said crisply.

'Got,' they both reported.

'Jungle Venom?'

'Sloshed on.'

'All right. You go and get ready in The Passion Flower Hotel, and I'll be meeting the Clients.'

So they sploshed off to the gym and prepared themselves in languorous attitudes, and I went to the gate and waited. The two Clients duly arrived, a bit late, and I took their money: two pounds, in large silver. Then I led them to The Passion Flower Hotel and started to usher them into their respective tunnels.

'You do understand,' I said sternly, before raising the flaps, 'what is involved in Category Two?'

'Touch: Entire Operative,' replied one immediately. He was a lanky youth with huge hands and a monster macintosh.

'Touch means *touch*,' I warned, 'not—'

'Don't worry,' said the other Client, 'we won't bite.' He was a bit spotty, but not (I thought) so spotty as to repel Janet.

'Very well, gentlemen,' I said. 'I will call you in half an hour.'

'Wacko,' said the lanky one. (They were all a bit common. I suppose with boys' schools, when you really come down to it, it is Eton and the rest.)

'Wacko,' echoed the slightly-spotty one faintly. They scuttled in.

* * *

I sat on the stage, in the pitch darkness of the enormous, alarming gym. I thought the best thing, as I was the only guard, was to sit tight and listen; and, besides, it was still raining.

After twenty minutes, one of the flaps shifted a bit. I dropped down to the floor of the gym and lifted it.

'You have another ten minutes,' I said. (One builds a business on a policy of fair dealing and ethical practice.)

'Yes, I know,' said Lanky. 'But it's all right.'

'You mean it's *not* all right?'

'No, it *is* all right—'

'Oh, good,' I said, mystified.

'But I think I'll come out now, if you don't mind.'

'I don't mind,' I assured him. 'Don't you mind?'

'No,' he said awkwardly. 'Actually I'd rather.'

Virginia was still in her chamber in the Passion Flower Hotel, and of course Miss Gaby de la Gallantine's Client was still with her. So, speaking purely socially, it was rather a difficult moment.

He sat on the edge of the stage, some feet away from me, and said, 'I think I'll wait for Tremlitt. That's the other chap. Unless you'd rather I went?'

'Certainly not,' I said politely. 'Feel free.'

'I say, thanks.'

So we waited. Ten minutes is a very long time.

Presently (after about one minute, also a very long time though not, of course, as long as ten) I said, 'I hope you were not dissatisfied with Mademoiselle Chantal?'

'Oh *no*,' he said, 'she was super.'

'Perhaps you were' – I didn't want to hurt his feelings, but it was important to know, for the future – 'embarrassed?'

'No, thanks awfully, no, not a bit. Well, yes, actually, to be honest, I was a bit, at first. But she was jolly good, you know, and being masked, and being, I suppose, sort of experienced ...'

'All our Operatives are fully experienced,' I said.

'*Exactly.*'

'But,' I said, 'something was wrong ...?'

'It just wasn't *quite*,' he said anxiously, 'what I'd banked on.'

He really was too polite. It was difficult getting what he meant out of him, but I had to go on trying, because of our commercial future. A viable enterprise must be aware of its customers' needs.

'I don't want to sound rude to Mademoiselle—to your *person*,' he finally said in answer to my probing but gentle questions, 'but ...'

'Please tell me,' I said. 'The Syndicate is here to help.'

'Well ... but it's embarrassing!'

'It's quite dark. We can't see each other Just think of me as a professional business contact. There is nothing personal.'

'Oh thanks, I say, you're awfully good ... Well, I was going by those *photographs*.'

'We have not released photographs of any of our Operatives,' I said.

(But it occurred to me, in a brilliant flash, that there might at some stage be quite a lot of money in doing so.)

'No,' he explained. 'I meant those magazines. Things like *Peep-Show* and *Peek* and *Peek-A-Boo* and *Peep-Girls* ...'

'I am not familiar with them,' I said coldly.

'Well, we all jolly well are. Till you started this marvellous idea it was all we *had,* those magazines. Ellis—you know Ellis?'

'On business, yes.'

'Yes, well, Ellis goes and buys them in the Charing Cross Road in the hols. Of course he looks so much older. And all the girls in the pictures have—hm hm hm ...' He tailed off in hopeless throat-clearing.

'Have what?' I asked impatiently. 'Piles? Spots? Cleft palates? Appendix scars on their tummies?'

'Oh no.' He giggled weakly. 'No, they have, well, quite large busts'

'Ah.' I understood it all.

Poor youth. He had fed his lust on these repellent booklets, and they all showed him pictures of models of low type with enormous bulbous bosoms. I can think of nothing more common than an enormous bosom.

'Mademoiselle Chantal,' I said, 'has one of the most elegant and admired figures in the profession.'

'Oh yes,' he said politely, 'I'm sure you're right—'

'But you would prefer an Operative with ...'

'Well, I *would* rather like to try with one who ...'

'Whose measurements were more generously ...'

'Yes,' he said happily. 'Have you got one? I've got another pound. Not with me, of course. But I can afford another go.'

'We can get the Operative you require,' I said positively. 'The Syndicate Will Meet Your Needs.'

* * *

Miss Gaby de la Gallantine's Client duly emerged, a minute or two after I shouted 'Time', and he and Lanky disappeared into the night. Janet's looked sheepish but happy, and Janet reported a quite reasonable degree of initiative.

'Mine was rather sweet,' said Virginia, 'but not really very keen.'

'Mine was rather keen,' said Janet, 'but not really very sweet.'

'You've done a magnificent night's work, both of you,' I said.

'And now we must drably creep back to our downy nests.'

'I hope we can,' said Janet.

But, as it turned out, we couldn't.

Chapter Twelve

Janet and I said goodnight to Virginia and shuffled softly to our dormitory. Janet was in front of me and she opened the door expertly: not a sound. We slipped in. It was dead quiet, except for breathing. Everything seemed fine. Janet crept away, across the room, to her own bed. I shut the door, utterly noiselessly, and turned, and was just about to tiptoe across to my own bed, when I was suddenly transfixed by a blaze of light.

'You monkey,' said Cordelia, in a low, accusing whisper.

'Ooh,' I squeaked, in fright and surprise.

Cordelia was sitting up in bed holding a torch as though it was a tommy-gun. I felt like a hoodlum in a film trying to escape from Alcatraz.

'My goodness, you're in trouble. I warned you.'

My mind raced. I was in trouble.

'I heard someone go out,' Cordelia said in her penetrating whisper, 'and I looked at your bed, and you've been an hour and a quarter! You are a silly pickle.'

'And in one,' I murmured brokenly.

I went over to her bed, trying to think of something. It would have to be good. Or this was the end.

She was wearing flannelly pyjamas with a pattern of rosebuds. The rosebuds looked ridiculous, stretched over her great biceps and her hundredweight of bosom.

Her hundredweight of bosom.

A wild idea came to me.

I sat down nervously on the edge of her bed, and whispered, 'I'm glad you're awake, Cordelia.'

'Fancy that,' she replied sarcastically. 'I bet you are, I don't think'

'Honestly. I've got a very important, urgent, private, personal message for you.'

'Oh yes? And I've got one for you, too. I'm going straight to Miss Abbott first thing in the morning.'

'Listen, Cordelia, please. I know I've broken the rules, but wait till you hear—'

'You can tell Miss Abbott.'

'I think you'll find you'd rather I didn't, when you hear this message Please listen.'

'Make it quick, I'm sleepy.'

'All right. Well. Have you—ever—been in love?'

'Ah, is *that* it? Assignations? A boy from the village? Oh Sarah, I never dreamed it was that bad, goodness, think of your mother!'

'Please listen,' I whispered urgently. 'You don't understand at all. I got a note from a distant cousin of mine at Longcombe. A friend of his is in a terrible state, because … this is true, honestly …'

'Come on, get cracking.'

'Do you remember the first eleven match against St Hildreth's? Last term? You scored dozens of goals—'

'Two,' said Cordelia.

'There was quite a big crowd, remember, Cordelia? And this friend of my distant cousin's was there. I don't know why. And he saw you. He watched you. And he's seen you since.'

'When?'

'He's bicycled over. Lots of times. All the way from Longcombe. And hidden in something, near the playing-fields. In the *bushes.* And watched you … just you. Lots of times.'

'Good gracious,' whispered Cordelia in a hushed, unbelieving way. 'Why?'

'He's fallen in love with you.'

'What awful piffle.'

'So *you* say. He can't work, he's going to fail his exams, he's been dropped from the rugger team, he's lost nearly a stone—'

'Needs a tonic'

'Yes,' I whispered cajolingly, 'you.'

'I never heard such disgusting twaddle.'

'My cousin,' I went on urgently, 'sent me this SOS to meet him. He said it was life or death. So I had to, even though it meant breaking the rules, a bit, and letting you down as our new pre—'

'Never mind that. What did he say?' And when Cordelia said this, hope dawned. 'Well, this friend of his really is in a terrible state. All those things I said.'

'Dropped from the team,' murmured Cordelia, impressed (I thought) by this tragedy. 'Lost a stone?'

'Nearly. Ten pounds. Just over ten pounds.'

'Gracious … What's his name?'

'I don't know. My cousin wouldn't tell me. He wants—well, obviously, he wants to meet you.'

'I couldn't possibly. I'm a prefect, Sarah. I'm in a position of *trust*.'

'I could arrange it all,' I said reassuringly. 'I've no doubt of that.'

'Well, I leave it to your conscience. Remember his exams. And the rugger team. And the ten pounds.' I finished.

'More than ten pounds … What does your cousin's friend say about me?'

'It was your figure he noticed first.'

'Oh … What dreadful rot, good heavens, I never heard anything like it. My *figure*?'

'I leave it to your conscience,' I said again, and undulated across the room and slid into bed.

* * *

Janet told the others about this epic conversation, next morning, in the History Library. (I was too modest to.)

'And at the end our Hockey Skipper was half way to The Passion Flower Hotel,' Janet concluded.

'No,' I said, 'only the beginnings of a first faltering step.'

'Dear God,' said Virginia, 'what a recruit'

133

'Don't count your Cordelias,' said Mary-Rose depressingly, 'before they're undressed.'

'Such a simple, straightforward request,' said Melissa thoughtfully. 'Two Category Two: Entire Operative. And what a lot of trouble it's caused.'

'That's life,' said Virginia. 'Innocently we drew lots—'

'Full of girlish eagerness—'

'The dear little bits of paper popped out of the dear little books—'

'By the way,' said Janet, 'what did you do with those dear little bits of paper?'

'Yes,' I said, suddenly very serious, 'Virginia? Mary-Rose? What did you do with them?'

'God,' said Virginia, 'I don't know. I think I put mine back in the book.'

'Oh Virginia! And you, Mary-Rose?'

'Well,' said Mary-Rose, looking frightened, 'I think I put mine back too. I can't remember. Anyway Virginia did it too.'

'Quick, quick, quick!'

We shot to the shelves and peered madly.

'Hey,' said Melissa, 'the books have gone.'

'They can't have,' I said, with mounting panic. 'Somebody's just moved them ...'

We searched all over the History Library. The books had gone. Somebody had indeed moved them; and with them those utterly damning ghastly dreadful fatal two halves of Ellis's letter.

'What exactly,' said Mary-Rose, after a long and terrible pause, 'did Ellis's letter say?'

'Quite enough,' I muttered.

'Oh dear,' said Melissa anxiously, 'oh bloody dear. What will you do, Sarah?'

They all turned to me. It is pathetic how dependent lesser people are in moments of crisis.

'I will cope,' I said as comfortingly as I could. 'Trust your Chairman.'

* * *

The deplorable creature who taught History to the babies was a Miss Trent, a sad female, with a mud-coloured bun high on the back of her narrow old head.

'Miss Trent,' I said the following morning during Break.

'Yes, Sarah?' she said in a frightened way.

'There used to be a book in the History Library which just by chance the other day I just chanced to want to look at—'

'Yes, Sarah?' she said, as though looking for a trap.

'A little book called *England In The Middle Ages: An Introduction For Junior Forms.*'

'Ah yes, quite a useful guide. Surely you are on to more advanced material, Sarah, in 5B?'

'Oh yes, Miss Trent But I remembered it had a very good account of the manorial system, and I wanted, well, I just by chance had a feeling I just wanted to look, you see, just to get a sort of general picture—'

I saw I was beginning to panic. I was glad none of my colleagues were there. But Miss Trent was too innocent to notice.

'How interesting, Sarah,' she said gravely. 'I think, you know, that a book of that kind is apt to be rather misleadingly superficial about a complex socio-economic phenomenon like the manorial system. After all—'

'I know, Miss Trent,' I said desperately, not having the time for a lecture on feudalism. 'The thing is, the book had disappeared. Every copy! I wondered if you knew—'

'Oh yes indeed,' she said. 'I have taken them all. I am introducing 3A to our medieval history.'

'3A.'

'The book is perfectly adequate for 3A. Problems which are in a sense sociological have to be simplified, indeed if you will, oversimplified, for—'

'Sociological,' I said brokenly, feeling the irony like a snakebite.

'I hardly know where you will find a copy at this moment, dear. 3A will have taken them off to their lockers.'

'Thank you, Miss Trent.'

'Not at all, Sarah. I am delighted to see you are interested.'

* * *

So we tried such members of 3A as we could identify. 3A are about twelve years old; consequently it is difficult (as with Chinese) to tell them apart. Some of these tinies had not yet got the book. Some had already done their devoirs and passed their copies on. One weepily admitted having lost hers, somewhere on the way to the dining-hall. One or two of the little green books we found, but without the incriminating bits of Ellis's letter.

'Anyway,' said Mary-Rose, after two or three anxious days of this, 'those dear little mites won't know what the letter's about.'

'They'll just throw it away,' said Janet hopefully. 'I expect it's already in the dustbin.'

'What they might do,' said Melissa in a worried voice, 'is show it to someone.'

'Someone like Cordelia.'

'Someone like Miss Abbott.'

'Oh mummy,' whispered Mary-Rose in horror, 'oh no!'

But after two or three more days nothing had happened. No bombs fell; no dread summonses came; no suet-pudding prefects called me out of classes. We breathed again.

'So what we must do,' I said, 'is get back to business.'

'Business being Cordelia.'

'Cordelia is our first vital problem.'

'Ooh,' said Mary-Rose.

'You must help, Mary-Rose. You're her chum.'

'Shall I talk to her?'

'You talk to her.'

* * *

And Mary-Rose, over the next few days, talked to Cordelia softly and often. We all hoped for the best.

Meanwhile I wrote to Ellis again, and said that it seemed that some Clients required, or would prefer, Operatives of special type, each to his personal taste We could not provide giants, midgets, albinos, or other freaks, nor would it be in accordance with our rigid professional standards to do so, but within reason The Syndicate would meet their needs.

He wrote back immediately, saying this was an excellent idea, and would be much appreciated by several Clients, including him.

I wrote back saying that Operatives to a special specification would carry a twenty-five per cent surcharge, owing to difficulties and hazards and expenses of recruiting.

He wrote back to say that was quite OK, and an extra five bob for what *he* wanted would be cheap at the price.

This was fine, and looked as though it might be a money-spinner But it meant we might have to recruit some very odd Operatives We hoped we would manage to, when it came to the point.

All this correspondence took time, but we unfortunately had time, because until we had some kind of certainty about Cordelia we were, as an enterprise, stumped.

Finally, after nearly ten days, Mary-Rose reported. 'She'll meet him'

'Brilliant Marvellous.'

'I played on her figure. You were clever to start that one, Sarah.'

'Oh no,' I said.

'She thinks, in her heart of hearts, that skinny girls and Vogue models and things aren't proper women. So she's not fundamentally the least surprised at Lanky's lamentable lust.'

'God,' said Melissa, grinning incredulously, 'our Hockey Skipper.'

'But does she realise,' I asked uneasily, 'what meeting Lanky is supposed to involve?'

'Well,' said Mary-Rose, 'I'm not sure. Sometimes I think she's absolutely with us. Sometimes not.'

'She gives nothing away to us,' said Janet. 'Not in the dorm she doesn't.'

'So it's really going to be assignation-with-Cordelia-night soon,' said Virginia. 'It's hard to believe.'

'It's fraught with peril,' I said. 'If she gets shocked or horrified by Lanky's eagerness, we're back where we were, only worse.'

'Brief Lanky,' suggested Melissa.

'Yes,' I said slowly. 'He's quite nice I believe we could.'

'He may be nice,' said Virginia a bit sourly. 'In fact I agree he is. But his taste is peculiar to the point of perversity.'

'Utterly totally ludicrous and a bit disgusting,' I agreed quickly (morale again). 'But there you are. The customer is always right. That is to say, in this case, quite wrong, Virginia, as we all know, but we have to proceed on the assumption.'

'Quite quite,' said Virginia. 'I wish dear Cordelia joy of him.'

'Whereas we,' said Janet, 'wish him joy of Cordelia.'

* * *

Our arrangements were subtle and complex.

I wrote to say that Client J6 (Lanky) could now be suited, in Category Two: Entire Operative at twenty-five shillings.

Ellis wrote back: Lanky was on.

So then Mary-Rose and I formed up, in a very girl-to-girl way, to Cordelia.

'He's lost another two pounds,' I said sepulchrally.

'He's just been kicked off the *second* fifteen,' said Mary-Rose, apparently close to tears.

'He bicycled over again yesterday,' I said. 'He watched you practising tackles on the lower hockey-pitch.'

'Ooh,' murmured Cordelia. And she blushed.

'The thing *is*, Cordelia,' I said, 'he's very passionate.'

'What do you mean, exactly, passionate?'

'He's in love, Cordelia,' said Mary-Rose softly. 'You know what men are.'

'What are they?' she asked innocently.

'Passionate,' explained Mary-Rose, a bit inadequately.

'Well,' I said carefully, 'I don't suppose he'll just want to sit and talk.'

'No,' agreed Cordelia immediately and surprisingly, 'I don't suppose he will.'

'He may want to make,' said Mary-Rose in a stifled voice, 'er, a sort of physical contact—'

'Yes,' said Cordelia.

'I hope,' I said, 'you will be kind, Cordelia. He has suffered.'

Cordelia stood up from the small, frail chair she was dangerously sitting on, and pulled down her blouse efficiently. It tightened over her immense front. I realised, with shock and a certain dismay, that she was expressing, in this simple movement, pride of womanhood. It was a bit horrifying. But it boded marvellously.

'I still don't know, do you,' said Mary-Rose afterwards, 'quite if Cordelia knows quite what's expected of her?'

'We must talk to Lanky very carefully,' I said.

* * *

And two nights later we did.

Lanky had arrived, by himself, a bit earlier than our usual hours of business. I took him to the gym, and Mary-Rose and I, very frankly, described the position. He was to be a sighing, desperate, lamentable lover: he had lost almost a stone, was about to fail his exams, and had now been kicked off even the third rugger fifteen.

'Oke,' he said. 'What happens if it doesn't work? Money back?'

'If it doesn't work it will be your fault She's psychologically prepared.'

'You mean sex-starved?'

'No, not sex-starved,' I said with distaste. 'Unawakened but ready to be awakened. But you must be gentle and considerate.'

'All the time?'

'Oh no. But to start with.'

'Oke.'

There was a rustle at the dark far end of the gym, by the main door, and Janet padded into our little circle of light, leading Cordelia.

Cordelia looked incredible. Heels. Lipstick. Cocktail-dress, near enough (I hoped it wouldn't baffle Lanky by its perplexing belts and zips). Heavy, heady whiff of Jungle Venom. (Clever Janet, I thought: its effect on Cordelia would be profound, regardless of its effect on Lanky.)

139

We all realised, I think, quite for the first time, that Cordelia was really rather handsome: quite a good and well-boned face, and a fine figure of a woman – carrying this, indeed, to the point of considerable exaggeration But this was what our Client had ordered. 'Here she is, your ideal.' I breathed dramatically.

Lanky clutched his hands together. 'My God,' he said throatily, 'I never realised ... I never knew ...' He lurched forward, and suddenly clutched both Cordelia's hands. 'You are very beautiful,' he muttered. 'Do you mind my telling you that?'

'No,' said Cordelia comfortably.

'Your hair, your eyes, your divine form—'

I signalled to the others and we faded away. As we slid out of the door of the gym, Lanky was breathing earnestly down Cordelia's ear.

'Wasn't Lanky bliss?' said Mary-Rose.

'He was overdoing it,' I said, worried.

'Cordelia didn't think so,' said Janet. 'Did you see her face?'

'No,' I admitted, 'I was so amazed by Lanky.'

'So was Cordelia,' said Janet.

'Frankly, I was amazed by Cordelia,' said Mary-Rose.

'Let's hope Lanky will be.'

'She beats those girlie-book photographs hollow.'

'Beats them concave.'

'But will Lanky get that far?'

'We'll know in half an hour.'

'Will Cordelia tell us?'

'Probably not. But Lanky will. I can't wait! Can you wait?'

'Barely, chums, barely.'

* * *

'Well?' we said to Lanky, as he loomed through the darkness in his huge white macintosh.

'Super,' he said briefly. 'Just, well, *super*.'

'Tell us.'

'I can't. It wouldn't be fair.'

'We,' I said, 'are The Syndicate. We arranged this to meet your needs. If we are to provide our Clients with a reliable and proper service—'

'Oh yes. I'd forgotten I'd *paid* ...'

'How divine,' said Mary-Rose. 'I call that high praise.'

'Yes,' agreed Lanky, 'I suppose it is, isn't it?'

'Was Mademoiselle Musette—?' I began.

'Is that what she's called? Musette?'

'Her professional name,' I explained.

'Musette,' murmured Janet. 'Divine.'

'She was,' I went on insistently, 'satisfactorily co-operative?'

'Yes!'

'Category Two?'

'Yes!'

'You didn't,' I asked sternly, mistrusting his tone, 'go into Category Three, did you?'

'Not this time,' he said, with an awful sort of high male giggle.

'Good gracious,' said Mary-Rose faintly, 'Musette ...!'

* * *

Some minutes later Janet and I slunk back, and went and whispered to Cordelia.

'Thank you,' she said, 'thank you.'

'Did you like him, Cordelia?' Janet asked.

'Ye-es,' said Cordelia, considering. 'He's very nice. But—'

'But—'

'He was terribly nervous'

'Can you blame him? He worships you, Cordelia!'

'That may be the trouble,' agreed Cordelia. 'He was awfully tentative—'

'Goodness,' Janet exclaimed in astonishment.

'Someone who was a bit less emotional and soppy about it all,' Cordelia said in a sensible, down-to-earth way, 'might be a bit more active.'

'Would you,' I said, amazed, 'prefer that, Cordelia?'

'Well, isn't that the *point*?'

'Yes,' Janet and I agreed simultaneously.

'Would you,' I went on, still amazed, 'like to meet someone a bit more—active?'

'I might.'

'The Syndicate,' I whispered confidently, 'Will Meet Your Needs.'

* * *

The Inner Council decided that Cordelia was really another Client. We were meeting her needs. So there was no need to give her any of the money. But we would, we decided, subsidise her to the extent of a free issue of Jungle Venom as and when required.

* * *

I wrote to Ellis again.

Dear Harold,

The Syndicate gathers that last night's Client was pleased with Mlle Musette. This is gratifying to us, since we endeavour at all times to give complete satisfaction.

Mlle Musette is now available, at special terms, as part of our regular service.

Awaiting your esteemed instructions,

We have the honour to remain,

S. CALLENDER

He wrote back by return of post.

Dear Sarah,

Musette sounds just my personal cup of tea. Category Three Type A which I think you call Nothing Barred Except. This is my personal cup of tea. Thirty bob plus 25 per cent makes 37/6 I think? I hope she is all my pal says, at that price.

'Dear God,' said Melissa, as we all read this together, 'Cordelia's in for it now.'

'It's what she wanted,' said Janet.

'But *Ellis*,' said Mary-Rose, who had never quite got over her horror at this sinister elderly boy.

'Active,' said Janet. 'What Cordelia needs.'

'Read on, Boss,' said Virginia.

Another man also wants a special request, which is an easy one I should think. It is Category Two: Entire Operative, the point being a blonde. Everything else as per standard, but definitely a real blonde. Can do?

We also have a Category One: Entire Operative batch. Can you cope with all this at one go?

Yours,

HAROLD

'A blonde,' said Virginia thoughtfully. 'I for one am dark.'

'Me too,' said Melissa.

'And I'm red,' said Mary-Rose.

'Auburn, dear. Or Titian.'

'Would you call me a blonde?' asked Janet hopefully.

'No,' said Melissa, kindly but firmly.

They all turned to look at me.

'How lucky,' said Melissa, 'we have a golden-haired blue-eyed boss-lady to fill this delicious bill.'

'Atishoo,' I sneezed. 'Damn, I still seem to be getting this cold.'

'Cold feet,' murmured Mary-Rose.

'You're not suggesting, are you,' I said in furious indignation, 'that I'm shirking?'

'No, Boss. But it's funny, isn't it, the way the lots have always gone?'

'Peculiar, yes. We've had this conversation. And I'm getting a cold.'

'Again? Hm?'

'What do you mean, hm?'

'Just hm.'

I looked round them. It was quite clear they all jolly well expected me to be the Special Operative, with Cordelia, at the next Passion Flower evening. And they would be very surprised, suspicious, and perhaps mutinous if I wasn't.

(You may wonder why I was so unkeen to be a Special Operative. I was, after all, just as feminine and frustrated as any of them. The answer is something I hate to admit, but must admit in the interests of accuracy. *I was scared.*)

So I changed tack.

'We're succeeding in business,' I said gravely and thoughtfully, 'just why, would you say?'

'Meeting needs.'

'Exactly. Cordelia for instance. Large bosoms were requested. We supplied the largest.'

'Quite the largest,' said Melissa.

'Mary-Rose, for instance, would not really have done.'

'No?' said Mary-Rose.

'You have a divine bosom, Mary-Rose, as we all know, which our Clients very much admire. But in point of sheer size you are simply not, frankly, in Cordelia's class.'

'No.' Mary-Rose admitted.

'Very well,' I went on coolly. 'A blonde is requested. I am, as you all quite correctly point out, more or less fairish. But according to our tradition of service and quality we ought to produce quite the blondest blonde available.'

'Such as?'

'As a blonde,' I said, 'I am in the second class.'

'In other ways first,' said Virginia politely.

'Perhaps,' I said. 'But purely in terms of just pure pigmentation, I am not as blonde as,Fiona Kerr.'

'Fiona Kerr?'

'Pity,' said Mary-Rose. 'Sarah's gone off her chump.'

'She is very, very blonde.' I pointed out.

'But *Sarah*—'

'I know,' I said. 'You can't see her in the Passion Flower Hotel.'

'Can you?' said Virginia.

'We have built a business,' I repeated firmly, 'on providing the best.'

'If you can do it,' said Janet, 'good luck to you. But you won't bring off another Cordelia. Not with Fiona Kerr.'

'No. A quite different approach.'

'*What* approach?'

'You'll see.'

Chapter Thirteen

Fiona Kerr was celebrated, in a school full of dismal wets, as the wettest. She had long, straight, pale hair, and pale, prominent china-blue eyes, and was in 5B, our form. She was in Mary-Rose's dormitory, and thus also under the pious eye of Felicity McBean.

(We had been lucky on the Homeric night of Cordelia's first appearance at The Passion Flower Hotel. Felicity McBean had migraines, just as you could guess from her appearance, and was away seeing a specialist in London So this solved her lesser problem – having *enlisted* Fiona Kerr – of getting her safely to the Hotel.)

Fiona Kerr was quite pretty. In fact anyone not knowing her would have said she was very pretty. But her dripping-wet, utterly insipid, goody-goody character made her revolting, and a most unlikely recruit for our operations.

So it was natural that my colleagues were surprised at my plan, and thought I would fail, and would have to be the special blonde requested by our Client.

But I knew something about Fiona Kerr that they didn't know, and that Fiona didn't know I knew. Sol sought her out, and said, 'Fiona!'

'Yes, Sarah?'

'You have a teddy-bear.'

'Oh … how did you know?'

'I know,' I said in a sinister voice, 'a great many things.'

'Don't tell anyone!'

'There is nothing at all,' I said more kindly, 'wrong or shameful in having a teddy-bear.'

'You—you don't think so?'

'I had one myself, a great many years ago, when I was three.'

'Oh ...'

'It shows a nice, gentle nature.'

'People would laugh ... It would be horrid if anyone knew ...'

'I promise not to tell anyone.'

'Oh, thank you, Sarah! Swear?'

'Yes. If ...'

'If what?' said Fiona nervously.

'I'll come to that. Before I tell you, I want you to imagine two things. One is that everybody in the whole entire school, *everybody*, knows that you have a teddy-bear, and sleep with it, and call it Cuthbert.'

'How did you know?'

'I know. And the other thing to imagine is Cuthbert being publicly cut into pieces with a great big pair of garden shears -in front of a lot of juniors laughing horribly.'

'No! Stop!'

'I won't do it, Fiona, I don't expect But in return you must do something for me.'

'Ooh,' said Fiona, nearly in tears.

'Something very nice indeed, which you will enjoy enormously, once you get used to the idea.'

I told her. It had an odd effect: she simply didn't believe me. She thought I was only making a horrible joke And when I managed to convince her I was serious, she grew horrified and weepy. So I said, softly, 'Poor Cuthbert.'

So she was not exactly a willing recruit, like the amazing Cordelia, but she was in We could, once again, meet needs.

* * *

The way I knew about Cuthbert is, I suppose, rather awful. But can anyone, honestly, resist a letter he finds lying about?

* * *

The Client who had ordered a blonde turned out to be blackish, or, at the kindest, a sort of dark khaki. He was Persian or Levantine and not sinister, as one might have thought, but rather sweet and pathetic, and shy, and respectful. It was obvious that he would never get to Entire Operative with the silly and ignorant Fiona Kerr, unless things were made very easy for him. Besides, one felt it one's duty, as host to a foreigner of colour, to be as friendly and hospitable as possible.

So I sent Virginia hurrying back from the main gates to the gym, where Mary-Rose was waiting with Fiona and Cordelia. My orders were that Fiona was to be Entire Operative all ready for The Client when he came. If Fiona objected, Virginia was to shake her head sadly, and say 'Poor Cuthbert.'

Business is business.

Ellis looked, unlike his friend, very sinister indeed. He had put something sweet-smelling on his thick black hair, and he wore a truly blood-curdling smirk.

He rubbed his hands. 'Musette, here I come,' he said vulgarly.

'Ellis—?' bleated a voice from the darkness.

'Oh yes, I'd forgotten you. Hey, Syndicate, we've had to change our arrangements, I hope it's all right. I think you were expecting a party for Category One—'

'Yes. Miss Gaby de la Gallantine is waiting to give her performance.'

'Of course, God, sorry. Look, they couldn't get out. Somebody talked—'

'Somebody talked?'

'Don't worry. You're not implicated. But they couldn't get out.'

'That is unfortunate,' I said coldly. The Category One party were to have been accommodated at a special party rate of two pounds seven shillings and sixpence.

'But this bloke has come with us.'

'Good evening,' I said to a shy shape in the shadows.

'Evening,' he simpered back.

'So,' said Ellis, 'could Miss Gaby do a Category Two?'

I thought quickly. Miss Gaby wouldn't mind, knowing Miss Gaby. And it was a pound. Or more.

'Do I understand that The Client is "specially requesting" Miss Gaby de la Gallantine?' I asked keenly.

'Ha, ha, yes, I see,' said Ellis. 'A jolly big eye for the main chance your Syndicate have got, haven't you? I don't blame you. Yes, all right. Twenty-five bob. All right, Itchy?'

'All right,' bleated Itchy.

'Accommodation may be rather a problem,' I said, 'but rest assured that The Syndicate Will Meet Your Needs.'

Money changed hands, and I conducted them to the Passion Flower Hotel.

Mary-Rose came forward from the darkness to report.

'Ingrid is ready in the Blue Room,' she reported crisply.

'*Really* ready?'

'Cuthbert did his stuff.'

'Thank you.' I turned to the khaki Client. 'This way, sir, please.'

Khaki disappeared into the left-hand tunnel under the stage, smiling politely and blinking his amber-coloured eyelids rapidly over his little black eyes.

'Musette is in the Mauve Room,' said Mary-Rose.

'That's for me,' said Ellis.

So we pushed him into the middle tunnel.

'Miss Gaby de la Gallantine,' I said to the Client Ellis had called Itchy, 'will entertain you in the Annex.'

'Annex?' asked Janet from the stage.

'The wings,' I whispered back at her.

'Uncomfy ...'

'We'll fix it up.'

So we rapidly fixed it up, with various drapes and bits and pieces; it would have been rather public by daylight, but lit by one sexily-dimmed torch, and from the body of the gym, it was sufficiently invisible.

Silence fell.

Virginia, Mary-Rose, and I crept to the end of the gym and whispered casually about indifferent topics. It was odd thinking about Gaby in the wings, Ingrid in the Blue Room, and Cordelia in the Mauve

Room, all in the various ways entertaining their various Clients at the same moment. It gave me a feeling of pride and achievement. The Syndicate was meeting needs. One listened for rustles and squeaks and screams, particularly from Ingrid; but for a long time the silence was total, until I went to the edge of the stage and called 'Time!'

Then there were rustles, of a jingly, male-reorganizing type. Itchy appeared, bashfully beaming, from the wings, and jumped floppily down on to the floor of the gym.

'Goodish,' he said.

Then Khaki emerged from the Blue Room tunnel, grinning and blinking politely exactly as he had when he went in. I had the feeling that he had been grinning and blinking in exactly the same identical way throughout the previous half-hour. It would be interesting to hear what Fiona thought about it all.

Finally Ellis appeared. He came out of the tunnel slowly, like a reluctant escapist, and straightened up. He was altogether ruffled and different. His smarmy hair was on end, and his smirking expression had disintegrated into a sort of drunken simper. It was fantastic.

The three of them left, almost without a word, and when we had seen them out of the gym we returned to collect our Operatives.

Janet was ready for us, sitting on the edge of the stage.

'OK?' I said.

'Dreadful,' she said. 'Ghastly.'

'Why? Too active? Not active enough?'

'Spots.'

'Pimples, you mean?'

'Putting it mildly. Every time he moved a scab shot off.'

'Not ... pus?'

'Ugh.' Janet really and truly shuddered. 'I want about nineteen hot baths with gallons of Dettol.'

'Ooh,' said Mary-Rose. 'Poor Janet. How beastly.'

'We can't have that,' said Virginia. 'Not fair to Operatives.'

'I'll deal with it,' I said. 'We'll lay down conditions of acceptance of Clients.'

'God,' said Janet, 'oh God, please do.'

Then Cordelia emerged, a bit wind-blown but otherwise placid.

'Well?' we all said. '*Ellis*?'

'Better than that tall one you produced last time,' she said, 'but not what I'd call *male*.'

'Good gracious,' said Mary-Rose faintly.

'Don't be too long getting back, Sarah. Or you, Janet. Remember I'm still your dormitory prefect.'

'Yes, Cordelia.'

And the extraordinary girl strode out.

'Does Cordelia know what's going on?' said Virginia.

'You mean about The Passion Flower Hotel?'

'And the money and everything?'

'She must,' said Mary-Rose.

'She can't,' said Janet.

'I don't think she does,' I said, 'and I don't think she'd better.'

'Well, I'm not sure,' said Virginia.

Nor was I, to be absolutely honest, and I'm still not.

'Where's Fiona?' asked Janet.

'Fiona!' I called.

A thin, keening voice came out of the tunnel: 'Clothes!'

'Put them on, stupid.'

'Mary-Rose took them away.'

'Oh, yes, so I did,' said Mary-Rose. 'Silly of me to forget.'

We managed to find them, and pitched them into the tunnel. After ages Fiona came out.

'Well, Fiona,' I said kindly, 'I expect you enjoyed it, really, didn't you?'

'It was silly,' she said.

'Hm?' said Janet, startled.

'I thought he was going to rape me—'

'Good gracious, why did you think that?'

'I couldn't think why else you'd have me lying in a tunnel with nothing on, and then a *black* man coming in—'

'Brown,' I said, 'almost a sort of gold.'

'What did he do, Fiona?' asked Virginia with interest.

'Nothing, really. It was silly.'

I gasped. Was Fiona going to turn out another Cordelia? 'Do you mean you'd rather he had done something?'

'Oh no,' she said, shocked. 'I was glad. But I still just thought it was just silly.'

'He must have done something.'

'Not much.'

'But what?'

'It's a secret,' said Fiona, like a spoilt little girl.

'Would you like to do it again, Fiona?' I asked.

'Not much. I think it's so silly.'

She hadn't, in fact, really understood. She was armoured by innocence. It was just as well.

'All right,' I said heavily, 'let's go to bed.'

* * *

I wrote to Ellis again.

Dear Harold,
The Syndicate's operations are, as you know, becoming more complex. In order to maintain our traditional high standards of service, and at the same time protca our Operatives from occasional distress, we enclose a form of application, to be sent by you on behalf of each Client.

Yours,
S. CALLENDER

This was the form:

THE PASSION FLOWER HOTEL AND NOVELTY THEATRE

FORM OF APPLICATION FOR SYNDICATE SERVICE

Client's name (or nom de plume)
Date of required assignation
Service required (tick which applies)

Category One:
>
> Above Waist Only
> Below Waist Only
> Entire Operative

Category Two:
>
> Above Waist Only
> Below Waist Only
> Entire Operative

Category Three:
>
> Nothing Barred Short of La Pénétration
> Nothing Barred

Is special Operative required? (tick which applies)
>
> Yes
> No

If Yes, state colouring preferred (tick which applies)
>
> Very dark
> Dark
> Medium
> Dark Red (Chestnut)
> Light Red (Titian)
> Ash blonde
> Nordic Blonde
>> Any Other (Please describe)

And state build preferred (tick which applies)
>
> Very Ample
> Ample
> Generous
> Medium
> Slim
> Sylph-like

Declaration to be signed by Applicant:

I faithfully promise that I am not suffering from any boils, abscesses, carbuncles, open or running sores, or poisoned wounds.

I further faithfully promise that I have had a hot bath within the last 72 hours, or since I last played any active Game, whichever is most recent.

I guarantee and undertake and swear not to reveal the existence of The Syndicate or its service, or the identity of any Operative, to any unauthorised person whatsoever, so help me God.

Signed

Note 1. No application will be considered unless accompanied by a properly signed declaration, as above.

Note 2. Applications must be received by Syndicate Head Office not less than two full days before requested assignation.

Terms – strictly cash in advance
'The Syndicate Will Meet Your Needs.'
'Actions Speak Louder Than Words.'
'Save Today The Syndicate Way.'

'We ought to get it printed,' said Melissa.

'Thousands,' said Mary-Rose, a bit avariciously.

'How? Do you think a printer would do it?'

'We will use our dear school mag,' I said.

'I don't think,' Janet objected, 'they'd print it either. Or are you going to get all those awful dreary literary sixth-form lot into the Syndicate?'

'My dorm-mates,' said Virginia. 'No. Not in The Syndicate. Too old.'

'We won't require the editorial staff,' I said. 'Just the presses.'

'You mean the Roneo machine?'

'That's it, dear.'

'Do we know how to work it?'

'One of us must join the staff, and learn, and teach the rest of us, and double-quick.'

'Actually, I've been asked to join,' said Virginia.

'*Have you?*' I asked bitterly. (I should not have accepted, personally, if asked to join the pathetic staff of the puerile *Bryant*

House Bookbag, but it was typical of the ludicrous way things are managed that Virginia should have been asked but not me.)

'I said no. But I'll change my mind, shall I, and say yes? Just to learn how to work the Roneo?'

'That's it, chum. Learn fast.'

She managed to get a lesson two days later (from one of her dorm-mates, a grim girl who wanted to be a journalist), and the following night, under appalling risks, we typed the stencil and then ran off a beautiful fat bundle of Forms of Application.

* * *

It worked very well. During the following fortnight we had several Special Operatives Requested, at our beautiful twenty-five per cent surcharge, which happened to fit members of The Syndicate, which simply meant a lovely bonus. It was a comfort, too, knowing that Janet's awful experience with Itchy was unlikely to be repeated.

But there were a few Special Operatives Required which meant a bit of recruiting to the Outer Division. One Client wanted a 'very ample ash blonde'. Choice was surprisingly limited, and we picked fat slob Jennifer Bostwicke, for whom ash blonde is a generous but tenable description but who is quite utterly undoubtedly very ample. She was no problem to recruit. It was only a Category One: Entire Operative, and we gave her five bob.

Another Client wanted a 'medium dark red' Our only red was Mary-Rose, and she was much more at the titian end. We had to recruit Virginia's elderly dormitory-mate Meg Lavington. We were baffled for a bit, till Mary-Rose had the good idea of asking Cordelia to talk to Meg. But Cordelia refused, saying it would be immoral. She is a most unpredictable girl. Then, most luckily, Virginia, who had the next bed to Meg, discovered that she kept a diary. She brought it up to date every single day, during Rest Period after lunch. Once we got hold of the diary we were home. It was easy. Meg was a Category Two: Entire Operative. She didn't seem to mind too much, after crying for a short while, and we gave her back her diary when we dismissed her.

Yet another choosy fellow wanted a foreigner: any foreigner. That meant Marie-Claude du Bruton. Marie-Claude was yellowish and fattish, but unmistakably foreign Luckily she was very cowardly, so threats of violence were all that was needed It was a bit distasteful. One had to keep reminding oneself that business is business.

* * *

Then an annoying thing happened. A Client called for a 'medium ash blonde' And they all looked at me. I looked back at them (it was in the History Library, of course, on a sunshiny morning) and there was a bit of a silence.

'You can't get out of it this time,' said Mary-Rose.

'I have not, at any stage, tried to get out of anything,' I said coldly.

'It is most definitely you, Sarah.'

'I'm not really *medium?* I said. 'I'm *slim.*'

'You're medium,' said Melissa. 'Beautifully medium.'

'Irresistibly medium,' said Virginia.

'And wildly, blissfully ash blonde. So lucky. I've always envied the Chairman her hair, haven't you?'

'Always,' said Melissa.

'He wants Category Three,' I muttered.

'But it's Nothing Barred Short Of,' pointed out Janet. 'Not Nothing Barred.'

'Lucky, lucky girl,' said Mary-Rose. 'You will be a woman.'

'Not quite,' said Virginia pedantically. 'But *very nearly.*'

'All except for La P.'

'Well, but,' I said desperately, 'I can't.'

'Why, Boss dear?' But I couldn't think of anything to say.

* * *

I waited in the tunnel, all dressed up in a dressing-gown and reeking of that filthy Jungle Venom. (Melissa had rather cattily sloshed nearly the whole of a new bottle over me.)

This couldn't happen to me.

I waited for a very, very long time: so long, that I assumed that the others had made some dreadful amateurish blob of the arrangements I usually handled. Perhaps I was let off. I began to feel a blissful flood of relief welling up.

And then, suddenly, I heard scraping and scratching noises, and footsteps, and then Virginia's voice saying: 'La Vicomtesse is waiting, M'sieur.'

'Thank you,' said a manly voice.

And Colin scrambled in – Colin, my first original contact.

I squeaked with surprise, and he crawled a bit nearer and said, 'Good heavens.'

'Hello, Colin,' I said nervously. I couldn't decide, suddenly at that moment, whether it made it worse or better having a *professional* relationship with someone I knew *socially.* I thought worse.

'Oh dear, good *heavens,*' he said. I suddenly realised he was shocked.

'Well, hullo,' I said weakly.

There was a silence. I could hear a bit of rustling from above. The others were listening! Beasts and traitors. I had never allowed it when I had been doing my proper managerial job.

'I didn't expect it to be you!' Colin said finally.

'No?'

'It makes rather a difference—'

'You asked for a medium ash-blonde.'

'Yes, but I didn't expect it to be you.'

'I'm sorry.'

'I thought you just ran it.'

'So did I,' I said bitterly.

'I've met your mother and everything,' he went on, still shocked. 'It makes rather a difference.'

'Yes.' I agreed.

'Of course I have paid,' he went on abstractedly. 'A hell of a lot— oh, sorry Sarah—a terrific lot.'

'I'll refund it,' I said immediately.

'Oh, no,' he said politely.

'Of course. The Syndicate is entirely totally scrupulously businesslike.'

'All right, then,' he said, a bit too soon.

'I'll send you a postal order.'

'Fine. Thanks. What shall I do, then? Shall I go away?'

'No. Stay a bit. Twenty minutes. We'll make a few creaks and crashes for the audience.'

'Audience?'

'Guards,' I explained. 'Lots of guards. Security.'

'Ah, good, I see. Well, Sarah, how are you? Having a good term? Not working too hard?'

'I'm very well, thank you,' I said conversationally (but we were whispering). 'And how are you, Colin?'

So we chatted politely for twenty minutes, and every so often one of us gave a sexy groan, or thumped about a bit, and eventually Colin crawled out.

I disarranged my hair madly, and hauled the drapes about to imitate the after-effects of uncontrollable passion in the poor old Passion Flower Hotel, and then sat still and listened.

'La Vicomtesse was to your satisfaction, M'sieur?' I heard Virginia say.

'Ah oui,' Colin groaned theatrically. I felt terrifically grateful.

'Nothing Barred,' I heard Melissa squeak, 'Short Of ...'

'Nothing,' said Colin throatily, 'short of nothing.'

They all gasped. I could hear their gasps, even in the tunnel.

'Really?' Janet almost shouted.

Then Colin walked away, and presently they hauled me out of the Passion Flower Hotel and sat me on the edge of the Novelty Theatre.

'Well?' they all said.

'An adequate Client,' I said easily. 'Very adequate indeed. Really, of course, I suppose I should have charged more ...'

'Charged more?'

'Then it's true?'

'Nothing Barred?'

'Oh Sarah.'

'Come along, children,' I said. 'It's your bedtime.'

Just before we split up, outside the bicycle-shed, to creep back to our various nests, Melissa said, 'Sarah—'

'Yes?'

'Wasn't it a dreadful risk?'

I knew what she meant, but I said, 'You were all guarding, weren't you?'

'Yes, we were. But I mean—supposing you had a *baby?*'

'My child,' I said kindly, 'I was not exactly unprepared.'

'Sarah!'

'I'm deliciously tired,' I said. 'Goodnight.'

* * *

They treated me with a new respect. It was divine.

Chapter Fourteen

The following day I almost had the overpoweringly convincing feeling that I *had* entertained Colin to a Category Three: Nothing Barred.

It made me feel sad to think of the short, bitter-sweet course our affair would run. One night of passion at The Passion Flower Hotel; quick, tender-brutal kisses, perhaps, at occasional parties in the country, and we would go our ways. One must face the transience of such relationships. One must be adult and (woman in a man's world) brave.

I tried to explain this to the others.

'How mature,' said Janet admiringly.

'It is what a *woman* feels,' said Virginia.

'A woman!' said Melissa. 'Goodness.'

'Do you feel,' asked Mary-Rose, 'like Eve?'

'I am still myself,' I explained to them gently. 'Changed, yes. More profoundly changed than you can, perhaps, imagine. But I am still the friend you knew.'

'Goodness—' murmured Janet.

Two days later (days in which I tried not to patronise my colleagues: days in which they could all *hardly wait*) I was surprisingly summoned to the Headmistress.

'Yes, Miss Abbott?'

She looked very grim indeed. 'You remember that some weeks ago I gave you an extremely serious warning.'

'Yes, Miss Abbott.'

'It seems you have ignored it.'

'Oh no! Miss Abbott.'

'No? Perhaps, then, you can explain a most peculiar letter which has come into my possession.'

'A letter?' I breathed.

In a horrible and vertigo-making flash I realised: she had got Ellis's letter – the one we had left in the book. It had Longcombe School on the letter-head. It was explicit and damning, and the end of everything. Some nasty little delinquent in 3A had found it and produced it, and it had got to this great gaunt desk in front of me.

'I have been somewhat mystified by this letter, Sarah,' went on Miss Abbott, sounding like a great iron bell tolling over a gibbet. 'It's implications were clear, but I refused to accept them. I refused, for as long as I could, to contemplate the possibility of such depravity on the part of a girl under my charge. However ...'

She paused. I wondered if I dared meet her eyes, but 1 decided I couldn't. I felt utterly, genuinely sick.

'However, I can no longer deceive myself. Your guilt is quite plain to me. No denial on your part will have any other effect than to add lying to the long and disgraceful catalogue of your offences.'

The letter started 'Dear Sarah'. I was the only possible Sarah. This was bad luck – it is not a rare name. But there the fact was. The letter could be only to me. So the old bag was right: there was no future in pretending not to understand ... 'Very well, Miss Abbott,' I muttered.

'Good. We are at last beginning to understand one another. 1 now require you to tell me everything. I demand a full and frank confession. I may say this, Sarah—your continued presence at the school is neither tolerable to me, nor, I think, profitable to yourself. Consequently you have nothing to lose and everything to gain by being honest and straightforward for once in your dealings with me.'

Nothing to lose, I thought. Everything to gain. *Everythmg to gain*, I thought giddily, and I suddenly had my wild, beautiful idea.

'Very well, Miss Abbott,' I said brokenly, 'I will tell you everything I know.'

'I am glad to hear it. I am listening.'

I tried to force a tear, feeling that a certain dampness about the eyes would increase the force of my story. No tear came, so I blinked a good deal to convey, I hoped, a pitiable smarting of the eyes – an imminence of weeping.

'I'm afraid,' I began carefully, 'I must confess to you, Miss Abbott. I have allowed myself to be used as a sort of—messenger, for, well, I suppose you would say immoral transactions ...'

'Go on.'

'Felicity McBean,' I said, 'knew I had a friend at Longcombe whom I met at a party in the holidays—'

'Felicity McBean?' exclaimed Miss Abbott. 'What nonsense are you talking, Sarah?'

'Felicity McBean,' I repeated, 'was the first to come to me with a— well, request. Margaret Rent on was the next, I think, and then most of the other prefects.'

'What is this lie? What is this disgusting rubbish?'

'Oh Miss Abbott,' I said earnestly, blinking like mad, 'yes, it is disgusting. If you only knew what I have seen ... But when prefects say they want to hold, well, orgies with, well, boys, and—'

'Gracious,' said Miss Abbott in a dreadful whisper. I looked up at last, very solemnly. She was staring at me as though I was Fluxx, *The Monster From The Fifth Dimension.*

'I suppose it's no good,' I went on a bit girlishly, 'trying to keep anything back—'

'No,' muttered Miss Abbott.

'Well,' I said terribly sincerely, 'I don't think *at first* they did more than, well, just take their clothes off, and, well, I believe the word is *neck.*'

'Neck,' said Miss Abbott mechanically. She was staring down at her blotter.

'And of course at first there were only about a dozen of them involved. But I'm afraid it didn't end there. I saw myself, well, I think the word is, well, *relations.*'

'Oh God,' said Miss Abbott, which I thought wrong of her, in front of a pupil. Then in a stronger voice she said, 'Sarah, this is entirely preposterous. You are trying, in a very despicable way, to get out of trouble yourself by implicating others.'

'It wasn't me that implicated them,' I said earnestly. 'They implicated themselves. They were terribly keen.'

'This is all a lie.'

'You said yourself, Miss Abbott, I have nothing to lose by frankness. I am being entirely frank. It is not easy.' I struggled with my voice, which I made shake up and down in a desperate way.

She stared at me, breathing heavily. Her eyes looked a little out of focus, in an odd way.

I began to feel a bit drunk with my story, so I ploughed on. 'I always thought,' I said in a terribly embarrassed voice, 'people did that sort of tiling alone. Just two of them, I mean I never realised they did it in a great sort of *party*.'

'Party,' muttered Miss Abbott.

'I was a bit shocked,' I said. 'I didn't know quite what to do I didn't dare come to you—'

'Why did you not come to me?' she almost wailed.

'I was frightened,' I said in a tiny voice. (I was only a young girl, after all, exposed to experiences which had appalled me but which I did not fully understand.) 'You had warned me, Miss Abbott, that I was being watched, and so on ... I was scared to come to you. So I wrote—'

'To whom?'

'Well, the Chairman of the Governors. And several parents. Mine, of course, and others. I felt I had to make this known, Miss Abbott.'

'When did you post the letters?' she whispered.

'I haven't posted them yet. But they're all stamped and ready. And an article for the *Daily Trumpet*.'

'Oh no ...'

'I believe they pay fifty pounds for a good story.'

Miss Abbott choked.

'You would, for fifty pounds ...'

'I wanted to give the school a really nice leaving-present,' I said. 'Something for the chapel. But I had no money. I thought the *Daily*

Trumpet would be glad to pay me fifty pounds. You see I felt I had a duty, Miss Abbott—'

'*You* speak of *duty?*'

'Oh yes,' I said. 'I don't want to sound impertinent, Miss Abbott, but parents and people have a right to know about this sort of thing. The discipline and moral atmosphere here is … well, there were about forty girls in the gym last night.'

'Forty girls? In the gym? Last night?'

'Yes, Miss Abbott. And about the same number of boys. They were dancing at first and then, well, I tried not to see. They made me keep guard in case anybody came.'

Miss Abbott looked down at her blotter. From under a pile of papers she drew a torn sheet of writing-paper. It was Ellis's letter. She handled it gingerly, as though it was contaminated. She looked at it and then up at me, seeming rather a lot older.

'What is Category Two, Sarah?'

'I don't know *exactly*, Miss Abbott. It is a phrase they all use. I think it means, well, *intimacy*. When they say Category One I think they mean just, well, necking with nothing on. I think that's what it means.'

'And,' she breathed in horror, 'Category Three?'

'I suppose, Miss Abbott, they mean one stage beyond, well, intimacy.'

'One stage beyond?'

'Yes, Miss Abbott.'

This flummoxed her. I didn't blame her – I couldn't imagine, myself, what it could be, but it seemed to suggest truly appalling experiments.

'Forty girls,' murmured Miss Abbott.

'I think it was forty-two,' I said with careful sincerity.

'You will give me their names.'

'Oh Miss Abbott,' I said pathetically, 'I can't do that. I am not a sneak. Besides, there were too many to remember them all, and anyway it was fairly dark, and anyway when people have nothing on it is not so easy to recognise them …'

She seemed to shrink and look inwards. (I suppose my revelations came as a bit of a shock.) I felt almost sorry for her.

I wondered if the letter bore out my fantasies: I seemed to remember words like 'stark naked'. It was important to see.

'Can I see the letter,' I asked softly, 'please?'

She didn't seem to hear. I picked it up. Of course it was only half, and it looked like this:

Dear Sarah,
Thank you for yours t
  I must say last night
somebody coming in is a
what was she doing? Anyway th
gory One. I hate to
cold out there
  We note you are tight
ments. High time if I may say s
like last night and we shall
  I have pleasure in in
Category Two: Entire Oper
This request is on the strict
be 100 per cent.

Yours,
H.

PS. I need hardly point
Category Three is called for
security which has got to be 100
badly, we will be

You

Utterly innocent. I was absolutely flabbergasted and thunderstruck. It could be describing a demure walk in the evening, or a cup of coffee at the Transport Cafe, or pen-friends getting together on the football pools, or any of dozens of utterly harmless and boring little crimes.

Category One and Two and Three could be something to do with exams or cricket-fixtures or botany or bird-watching.

Or it could all be a sort of unofficial but serious-minded poetry club, or going in for crossword-puzzle competitions together, or collecting autographs, or swapping stamps.

But of course it was a bit late to think of all this now. I had got the whole 6th Form and most of the 5th having wild pagan orgies of the most depraved kind with the great male animals of Longcombe School.

Well, that was the position. I must make the best of it.

'Miss Abbott?' I asked politely

She said nothing, so I went smoothly on.

'Have I your permission to post those letters now?'

'No!' she barked, coming suddenly to life. 'You are to go and bring them to me at once.'

'I don't know exactly,' I said carefully, 'quite where they are at the moment. It may take me a little while to lay my hands on them. But if it is your wish I can promise to burn them all.'

'All,' she muttered.

'Except the one to the *Daily Trumpet*. I expect they will send a photographer down. You see I really would like to buy something nice for the chapel.'

She looked me in the eye and I could see she was beginning to understand.

'I think you will agree, Miss Abbott, that I am really not honestly personally to blame, except for being *led* ...'

She made a groaning noise, which I could not interpret.

'Also, you may not agree with me,' I went on anxiously, 'but I don't think the girls more directly involved than I was are really vicious either. I mean they lost their heads. I mean it was a sort of craze. I mean I don't think a lot of them knew what they were doing. I mean if even you had been there, Miss Abbott, I truly believe you might have ...'

She looked at me in a stunned way, and I saw I was going too far.

'What I mean is,' I said firmly, 'I don't truthfully and honestly think they will do it again.'

'They will be most stringently punished,' said Miss Abbott in a frightening whisper.

'Oh dear,' I said. 'I think after all it is my duty to send those letters to all the parents.'

She looked at me again, and I could see that at last she fully understood. It says much for the tact of the English Upper Classes that we both managed to avoid using the word blackmail.

'I give you my word of honour,' I finally said, 'that I won't tell a soul about this, ever, even after I've left.'

'Except,' I added softly, 'the *Daily Trumpet*.'

I must admit I did have the wild hope that I could get her to give me fifty pounds, instead of the *Daily Trumpet*. But I could tell that she was not keen on this idea, so I thought it best to abandon it. In the end all I got was a sort of general oblivion and amnesty, and for me personally a safe-conduct out of the school. I wasn't being expelled. She was just writing to my father to suggest that my particular needs could be better catered for elsewhere.

I suppose, in the circumstances, this was better than it might have been. And as far as money went, I did have my share of The Syndicate profits.

* * *

Two days later the whole of the Upper School was given a curious lecture. Miss Abbott hinted at all kinds of furtive evils, and talked about the horror and grief of parents. She said that after deep thought and prayer she had decided to take no further action, on the understanding that nothing of the kind ever occurred again. But she clamped down like mad on rules and bounds and hours, and announced a new and very strict system of discipline. So I was glad I was leaving – the operations of The Syndicate would become virtually impossible.

Quite what all the other girls made of this I never knew. I am afraid poor Cordelia must have felt it dreadfully.

* * *

The liquidation of The Syndicate was a poignant business. We did not talk much as we parted. There was nothing to say. And talking would have been difficult. So we rolled away in our various cars, and it was the end of an epoch.

Now I am to go to Switzerland, to a school near Lausanne. Then I shall finish in Paris, or possibly just London. Then I shall have to come out, and be a deb. Perhaps after that I shall go to Oxford, and then have a job in London.

All these places will offer me scope, I am sure, for my special talents. The end of The Syndicate is sad, but the future is exciting.

What is the best equivalent in Swiss French, I wonder, for Passion Flower Hotel?

Bad Bet

Mathew Carver is a successful Kentucky bloodstock breeder and racehorse owner with a considerable reputation. He is also a member of a syndicate consisting of men significantly richer than himself. Through him the reader is immersed in the world of racing from bloodstock sales at Newmarket, to the classic countryside of Normandy, the Bluegrass of Kentucky and the mansions of Virginia. Racing's aristocracy and its hard men, the touts, the fraudsters, the stable lads, tipsters and jockeys all provide the action and the sometime dubious underlying morality associated with the many sub-plots that develop. And Mathew himself is pulled in many different directions, not least by the three women in his life, two of whom love him and his wife who hates him. There is an extraordinary array of characters involved, and Longrigg's deep knowledge of racing is apparent as he weaves together the passion, disasters, hopes, triumphs, tragedies and humorous interludes that befall them.

Albany

Leonora Albany's great-grandmother harboured an astonishing secret. It seems that Leonora is the sole legitimate descendant of Bonnie Prince Charlie – and by rights, the Queen of Scotland. The seventeen-year old's pursuit of truth leads her to a path strewn with danger, violence and an unspeakable murder. Laura Black brings to life the struggles of an extraordinary adolescent in her fight to remain unconsumed by title and privilege. Mystery and suspense surround every character in this spellbinding tale of intrigue.

Praying Mantis

Victoria Courtenay is beautiful, charming to the core, although this is almost wholly affectation as she has an underlying ruthlessness in which she uses her looks and manner to obtain whatever she wants. Indeed, it goes much further as she has a thoroughly evil streak which drives her to lure people in and then strike, as a praying mantis. She is determined to get her way, with family, friends, and lovers … This novel is one of psychological suspense at its best and is full of surprises.

ALSO BY ROGER LONGRIGG

Necklace Of Skulls

Lady Jennifer Norrington, Colly and Sandro travel to India to uncover a drug-stealing operation which develops into something altogether more horrible and frightening. Jenny is caught and used as bait for the others by the perpetrators of a long series of religious murders that was thought to have been stamped out in the nineteenth century, but as an organisation still survives. This wholly credible tale is set against exotic backgrounds and contains the kind of detail readers have come to expect of Drummond. It is a true suspense novel in all of the best traditions, with plot and sub-plots and many surprises.

Paper Boats

The proceeds of a wage robbery come, by mistake, into the hands of Gregory Pratt as he sits on his commuter train. Gregory lives, with his father, in deprived circumstances in an old mansion which is converted into a form of commune for distressed gentlefolk. Gregory struggles with his conscience over the money, but his father is certain; no one will suffer if they apply the find to their own purposes, and those of their neighbours. This is a story of high comedy, shrewd observation, and an exciting read from cover to cover.

Snare In The Dark

Dan Mallett usually keeps one step in front of the police and authority in the west-country village where he lives. Dan goes out one night to poach pheasants, and it is on that night that Major March's gamekeeper is shot dead with an arrow. Knowing he will almost automatically be blamed, he disappears whilst devising a plan to identify the real villain.